THE DRAGON BOX

The Dragon Box

Second Edition

Rhett DeVane

Tallahassee, FL

This is a work of fiction. Names, characters, places, and incidents are either the product of the author's imagination or are used fictitiously. Any resemblance to actual events, locales, or persons—living or dead—is entirely coincidental.

Copyright © 2024 by Rhett DeVane

All rights reserved worldwide. No part of this book may be reproduced in any form or by any means, electronic or mechanical, including photocopying, recording, or by any information storage and retrieval system without written permission from the author or publisher. Exceptions apply only to brief quotations contained in critical articles and reviews.

No generative AI was used in the creation of this text or artwork.

NO AI TRAINING: Without in any way limiting the author's exclusive rights under copyright, any use of this publication to "train" generative artificial intelligence (AI) technologies is expressly prohibited.

Second Edition publication date: March 2026

ISBN (Paperback): 979-8-9885159-3-7

Library of Congress Control Number: 2026935093

Published by:
Happy Cat Press
Tallahassee, Florida
www.happycatpress.com

Author website: www.rhettdevane.com

In memory of my dear friend Peggy Kassees, Master Cosantóir, who helped me see dragons everywhere.

A special thank you to my friends and family for listening to endless musings about dragons. And especially to the dragons from every color clan that allowed me into their fascinating world.

CHAPTER ONE

A green garden lizard perched on a spiked leaf dappled with pinpoints of moisture. I could step outside and hold out my hand, let it sit on my palm. I'm not scared of reptiles—snakes, frogs, or lizards. Weird for most girls, so I've been told. The creatures like me. Don't know why.

The lizard's sides pulsed when it breathed, then two long slits opened up and tiny wings popped out. The head changed too—from rounded to jagged with wiry spikes at the crest. The creature grew to five times its size, then turned dark as charcoal, rose up on its back legs, and unfurled its wings. Its steely eyes stared at me, like I was something it hated. A slender puff of smoke curled from its lips. With one front leg extended, it reached toward me. Neither the screen nor the window glass stopped it, and the talons wiggled in the space between us as if they beckoned me to dare step closer.

"Yikes!" I lunged backward, slamming into the rocker where my brother sat.

"Hey! Get off!" Zach gave me a push. "What's the deal?"

I regained my balance before I stood, once again facing the window. "Did you see that?" I glanced toward my aunt and brother, sitting side by side in the sunroom rockers. A flicker of shock passed across my aunt's face and vanished so fast, I wondered if I had imagined it.

"See what, Aidan?" Zach said. "You're acting all stupid."

I turned and focused on the creature, blinked a couple of times to make sure my vision was working right. The dark dragon pulled back its clawed foot and morphed into an ordinary green lizard extending the rosy skin on the underside of its neck, looking for a quick meal. It eyed me, winked, opened and closed its mouth, and slipped into deep leaf cover. "Oh... nothing. Never mind."

Was I the only one who saw dragons pretty much everywhere? But this one was different than others I'd seen—or imagined. Not colorful and friendly. The way it had glared at me made the skin on my neck prickle. If one of those talons had reached my skin—I shuddered.

I slid my purple paisley tote from my shoulder and plopped it onto the floor next to my brother's battered duffle. Something metallic clanged to the floor.

"Dropped your watch, honey."

"Oh..." I bent down and scooped up my watch. "It does that a lot."

"We better try to get by the repair shop while you're here and have that clasp fixed or you'll lose it. Can't believe your mama lets you wear it like that. It's one of the few things left of your great-great Grandmother Ivey's." She smiled. "My grandma. You'd have liked her. She had the Irish red hair, same as you and me."

The watch was a piece of jewelry that had floated to me through time, as Mama liked to put it. I snapped it onto my wrist and gave it a tug to make sure the clip held. The gold band was rubbed dull, and the crystal face looked like a spider had spun a web across it. Two triangular green stones nestled between the links closest to the dial. I never pass by a jewelry counter without stopping to look for the same green stones, yet I'd never seen any like those on the Ivey clan watch, a mystery for sure. I loved, loved, loved the old watch, and took a minute to carefully wind it every morning, first thing.

Aunt Neece cradled a wooden box in her lap. Her real name is Denise, and she's really my great aunt, but that's too much to say. She didn't look like her usual bubbly fun self. Instead, little worry lines etched around her eyes and mouth. And she was pale. "Now looky here, both of you." Aunt Neece patted the lid of the box. It was no larger than the one holding my new cheerleading shoes, except it looked like some sort of fancy jewelry box. "You may *not* play with this unless it's raining."

"What's so special about a dumb old box?" Zach drummed his fingers on the rocker's arm. "What's inside it anyway?" He reached out a hand, but Aunt Neece stopped him before finger one touched the box.

"Don't even *think* about opening it now. Not until it rains." She said it all Southern-fried, like *RAY—uns*.

Zach jiggered in his chair. "But why? I don't even *like* rain. That's all it does. Rain, rain, rain!"

"Well, now you have something to do when it rains."

"I already do. My video games."

"This box is better. Believe me."

Enough blabbering about rain! Wasting time. The imagined dark dragon/lizard wasn't the only thing disappearing from my life. My summer vacation was dwindling by the second.

I took a couple of steps back into the kitchen and consulted the rooster-printed calendar on the refrigerator. The fifth of August, only two sad little weeks before Zach and I had to return to school back home in Lake City, to the *exact* same school Mama and her sister Sarah went when they were kids. And just like them, Zach and I stayed a few days at "Camp Neece" in Tallahassee, Florida, at the end of each summer. Still... only four days this time, a little shorter than usual. And Aunt Neece seemed grouchy. Not usual either.

My whole family was definitely stuck in a rut. Only, this year, I had other things I'd rather do. Like making more moolah babysitting to buy the pair of Miss Me jeans I spotted online, or taking off to Daytona Beach with Olivia and her mother for one final jaunt with my cheerleader friends before school started back. Camp Neece was all right for Zach, but I was too old.

"Aidan and Zach." Aunt Neece placed the mystery box on the wicker table next to her rocking chair. She stood up and propped her hands on her hips. "Been a year since you've stayed with me. Let's review the rules." She held up one hand and counted with her fingers. Her silver ring caught the light with its glittery green stone like the ones on Grandmother Ivey's watch. "You must make your beds each morning, help with the dishes, hang up your wet towels so they don't turn sour, and brush your teeth after each time you eat." Her crayon-red hair stuck up, reminding me of the scarlet birds that visited the feeders outside of the sunroom: cardinals. We covered bird identification during a "teachable moment" on our last trip to Camp Neece. There were always a lot of "teachable moments" at Camp Neece.

I combed my fingers through my own long hair, darker than Aunt Neece's, kind of chestnut-colored, but still reddish in the sun. My brother got stuck with plain old blond. Only the girls in my family had the redhead genes, and even that skipped a generation.

I reached over to smooth the cowlick at Zach's forehead. He pushed my hand aside and groaned, probably his comment on the tooth-brushing rule. He brushed his teeth, sure, but not as much as I did. I have braces and I could make a sandwich with the food stuck around my teeth after a meal. Yuck. I was no stranger to a toothbrush, though it took me fifty-five forevers to thread floss between all of the wires.

"Dirt and grime belong outside, *not* in my house, and *not* on your teeth," Aunt Neece continued, her words coming out in snips.

What was up with the new, stern Aunt Neece? Maybe she was just cranky from the heat.

Zach groaned again, louder and longer, and flailed his arms. He's not one for rules. I'm not either, but I'm almost thirteen, in two months, and he's only ten. I've learned to cope, and sometimes go around the rules.

"Why are you pulling the Mr. Drama routine?" Aunt Neece wagged the fourth finger at him, the one she'd held up for tooth brushing.

Zach dropped his arms with a loud smack against his sides. "We're not going to have gums left. We eat all the time."

I let out a chortle, then stuffed it when my aunt didn't laugh.

True enough, though. Breakfast, snack, lunch, snack, dinner, still more snacks. Daddy said he was surprised we didn't figure out how to eat in our sleep. Except, that was the old me. I tried to watch it more now. Had to fit in my new cheerleading skirt. And those ninety-nine-dollar skinny jeans. Not to mention how much grief I'd get from Olivia the Perfect, head of the squad and expert on everything, if I gained a single ounce.

Something gurgled, low like a small chuckle. Had it come from the box? Zach and I exchanged glances. "So what's up with that thing?" I asked.

"This—" she swept one hand through the air like a circus performer, "—is a Rainy Day Box." Aunt Neece nodded once, as if we should know what a Rainy Day Box was, for heaven's sake, and why it was special. Adults were so weird sometimes.

Strange, I'd been to Aunt Neece's many times, and I'd never seen the little chest. I moved closer and floated my fingertips over the carved top. Aunt Neece didn't try to stop me. The wood gave off a crackly kind of energy, not quite a shock. I jerked my hand back, looked to my aunt. Her eyes were round, then they weren't, just that fast. I smelled fire, as if a gust of something burning had seeped into the sunroom. A hint of decay, too. As quickly as the dragon I saw—or imagined—the odor vanished.

"Did you get it at one of those old-timey stores you like?" I asked.

"No. It's been in the family for generations. Passed down." Her shoulders drooped, like thinking about the box made her tired. She never let *us* slump like that, always carried on and on about the "glowing benefits of good posture."

Rows of jewels—blood red, deep blue, and emerald green—outlined the edges of the box. Real? Probably not, but they glittered more than any fake stones I'd ever seen. Odd carvings and scratches covered the top and sides. Wouldn't it be something if Aunt Neece let me have it? I would polish it and put special treasures like my journal inside, so Zach couldn't snoop and make fun of the dragon stories I scribbled. Shouldn't be obsessed with all of that, but I was, and my journal held a private place for my wild fantasies.

Zach's blue eyes shone. He wanted it too. What would he do with such a beautiful thing—use it to store the dumb baseball cards he and Daddy collected? He already had a plastic container for those.

Kaboom! A loud clap of thunder shattered the air. All three of us jumped. Zach grabbed my arm. Aunt Neece said, "Whoop!" and held one hand to her chest like she was having a heart attack. "One one-thousand, two one-thousand, three one-thousand," she counted. Lightning flashed. "That strike was three miles off. Listen for the rumble first, then you start your count, one-one thousand, two one-thousand, until you see the flash. Each second means one mile between you and the lightning strike."

My brother shot me a confused look, shaking his head like he does when something doesn't sound just right.

Aunt Neece's timing seemed off. But why would I question my great aunt, the family's official climate wizard? She watched The Weather Channel like it held the meaning of life.

Zach, on the other hand, had no such reluctance. "Are you sure, Aunt Neece?"

Aunt Neece shrugged. "Maybe I have it backwards. I've been a little flustered lately."

"Oh no. Rain!" Zach pointed to the wide elephant ear plants, jittering and dancing with the pelting drops. First, a few. Then a whole bunch, until the back yard looked fuzzy and soft around the edges. I liked the way rain did that.

Dark greens, then some lighter tones, to add depth to the scene. I fixed the view in my mind so I could use it in this year's art class. Only, I'd add a dragon. Maybe like the one I'd seen, or *thought* I'd seen, on the leaf. Watercolors would work best. The shades were more transparent. Guess I could paint something else, but dragons seemed to emerge from the tips of my brushes onto the paper all by themselves, and I let them. When I finished, the new painting would hang in my room next to the others in my private dragon gallery.

In the cloud shadows overhead, a figure took shape. First a head topped with spikes, then wings, a thick body, barbed tail, and four sturdy legs armed with clawed feet. It descended, landing close to the house. Silver glowing eyes with black slits for pupils focused on the sunroom. Evil hovered around it like an aura. I squeezed my eyes shut. When I opened them, the yard puddled with water, nothing else.

Yet Zach and Aunt Neece sat in their rockers, oblivious.

"I'm playing video games. Nothing else to do now since it's raining." Zach left the chair rocking and aimed toward the stairs, to the second-story room we always shared when we visited. Aunt Neece promised we'd each have a bedroom next year, after she cleared some boxes from the attic. It was a great little space with a treetop view. I planned to call first dibs on it. Age had to outrank bratty brother at some point.

Aunt Neece jumped up and planted her hand on the top of Zach's head and turned him around in one easy motion. He kept moving his feet like a car stuck in mud with the wheels spinning.

"What? Why can't I go inside?"

She set the box on the rocker cushion. "That's what the box is for, remember? Rainy day entertainment."

"What's in there? A Nintendo? An iPad?" Zach danced from one foot to the other. My brother: the wiggle-butt. As for me, I'd rather not spend my time on video games. I tear him up when it comes to word games and crossword puzzles. I kind of hoped something like that was in the box.

Aunt Neece gazed at the box and her eyes went all misty and faraway. Had to be more to this than some box of toys. I'd be up for most anything, to steer my mind away from visions of dark things.

"You kids stare at a computer screen too much. It's turning your minds to mush. Day like today is tailor-made for the Rainy Day Box." Aunt Neece turned around and headed for the living room, calling over her shoulder. "Entertain yourselves for a while. I'm going to watch My Show."

Her "show" was a soap opera. Aunt Neece and practically every lady in my family tuned into the same program; Daddy called it "The Young and the Rest of Y'all." Even people who were at work made sure they recorded it for later.

One thing for certain: Zach and I didn't interfere with Aunt Neece's show. But that also meant she wouldn't interrupt our time with the strange box.

The Rainy Day Box sat on the rocker, gently pitching back and forth, teasing us with its secrets.

Zach turned to me, all pouty. His bottom lip poked out far enough to be an umbrella for his chin. His rear cocked at an angle. Outside, the thunder boomed. I counted, "one one-thousand," but before I could say *two*, a bolt of white light hit so bright and loud, Zach and I dove behind the rocking chairs.

"That was close." My chest fluttered. I shot a wide-eyed look at Zach. We waited. In a couple of minutes, lightning flashed again, not as loud. I counted, "One-one thousand, two-one thousand, three-one thousand, four—" before the grumble of thunder.

"Doppler radar shows it socked in for the rest of today," Aunt Neece called from the living room.

Zach crawled from behind the chair. "What's 'socked in' mean?"

"Means it's going to rain for a long, long time." I rose and stood in front of the rocker where the box waited. Although I wasn't touching it, my stomach quivered. I reached one hand out. My skin prickled with electricity. I pulled my hand back again.

"Bet whatever's in there is dull, dull, dull," Zach said. He liked to repeat things three times for emphasis, a quirk he copied from me.

As he chanted the last *dull*, a faint scent wafted from the box, a blend of smoke and something foul, the same thing I'd smelled moments before. Zach picked up the box and clamped his teeth together when the clasp wouldn't budge. "Dumb thing's stuck."

The lid stayed closed, but the smoke smell grew stronger. I grabbed the Rainy Day Box from his hands, ignored the electric pulse snapping the hairs on my arm, and yanked until it flew open.

CHAPTER TWO

A burst of hot air stung my cheeks. I dropped the box onto the floor and waited for flames to lick the wood and set the rug on fire. The odd smoke scent hung in the air, then faded. The top of the box gaped open, but a haze swirled around the box, its own little greenish cloud. I backed up and held up a hand to stop Zach. "Don't touch it!"

Like always, my little brother didn't listen.

Zach reached in the box and brought out a plastic sword, the one-inch kind they put in kids' fast food meals with the barely-burger and not-so fries. He tossed it back in the box, then rummaged through the rest of the contents, picking up a marble, a worn set of playing cards, a small stone, and a glittery pink fairy wand.

I sat cross-legged by him on the floor. I picked up the fairy wand. "I haven't seen one of these since I was four and used to play dress-up."

"This is just old junk." Zach gave the box a shove. If it didn't beep, flash, or shoot pellets, my brother couldn't be bothered. Obviously, a little stinky smoke wasn't nearly dramatic enough for him.

"Got to be something good in here." I peered in, picked up a figurine carved from light green stone—a tiny dragon with emerald eyes. The same buzzy energy pulsed from the stone—made me feel wackadoo—like I could laugh and cry at the same time. "This is kind of cool. Wonder what it is?"

Zach grabbed it from my hand and gave it a quick once-over. "Ah, it's nothing." He pitched it over his shoulder.

A burst of white light blinded me. A fern stand toppled to the floor, and a scraping noise sounded from the ceiling. Two of the rockers slid toward the wall, pitching back and forth. I blinked to clear my vision of the little flash spots. I leaned back my head to take in the creature that towered at least four feet above us, bigger than a draft horse. I rubbed my eyes. People in stories are always doing that, rubbing their eyes when they don't know what to make of what they are seeing, and I sure didn't.

The creature's scales ranged from pale mint to lime around its neck and mouth, to moss and emerald across its belly. The ridge from its crest to the tip of its spiked tail was such a dark shade of green, it appeared black. And those eyes! Like green cat eyes with flecks of gold, except the pupils were inverted triangles instead of round. In all of my paintings of dragons, I had gotten the details correct, even the wiry little chin hairs and the double top eyelids.

"Jeez-O-Pete," Zach whispered, staring too.

And where was Aunt Neece? She usually hustled in when we crashed anything. Her snores sounded from the den.

Don't know why, but Zach picked up the tiny sword again. It sizzled and snapped like Rice Crispies splashed with milk and grew to a gazillion times its size. Zach grabbed the sword with both hands, struggling to wave it at the creature standing a few feet from us. I started to holler for Aunt Neece, but the bewildered look on the being's face stopped me.

"Put down the sword, Zach. You're scaring it."

Zach jabbed the air. "You think *it's* scared?" The sword made a low humming noise. My little brother's gaze roamed the sunroom. He propped the sword on one hip and reached into the box for the rock. Ah, a weapon for both hands. *So* Zach. As soon as it cleared the rim, the pebble swelled into a stone as large as a bowling ball. Zach teetered, trying to hold it in one hand and the sword in the other.

The dragon glanced from the sword to the rock. The spikes above its eyes crimped together. Smoke curled from its nostrils, yet I felt no fear. "Just put down the sword, Zach. P-please."

The dragon took a deep breath. Its shiny green chest expanded and the scales stood up.

"It's gonna fry us like a chicken nugget."

"Just do it!" I snapped.

Zach frowned at me, but he lay down the sword. It swirled, shrank, and turned to plastic. What the heck?

The dragon exhaled and the scales flattened back to sleek armor. "Oh, thank you *ever* so much. I hate violence." Its lips curled up in a dragon version of a smile: a little creepy. Its breath smelled like it hadn't brushed after any meals or snacks. The odor of boiled eggs. I breathed through my mouth.

"Um, it talks," Zach said.

I took my eyes off the dragon long enough to fire a *no-kidding* look at my brother, although it astonished me, too.

Zach put down the rock too. It shriveled back into a pebble, no larger than a dime. The dragon smiled wider. None of the dragons I'd ever seen in pictures smiled, nor did the two I thought I saw earlier. They snarled with sharp-toothed ferocity and bellowed fire that scorched entire villages. Maybe it was as I suspected. Dragons weren't so bad.

"I thought you were going to..." Zach inched toward the dragon, "you know... eat us."

Way to go, Zach. Give it ideas! I flashed a you're-a-moron look at my brother.

The dragon drew its lips into a straight line. "Why would I do that?"

"Dragons eat people, duh...!"

I widened my eyes at my little brother. Thanks again, Mr. Obvious. Always firing off like he knew everything.

"Lies. Simply lies!" The dragon shook its head. "I haven't, not once, eaten a human. Ugh! Now I *love* fish. I like most vegetables. Except tomatoes. Never developed a taste for them." It held up one talon. "I absolutely and completely adore spaghetti sauce, and it's made with tomatoes, but I don't like chunks of them. I know that's bizarre. But there you go." The dark green crest above its head scraped the ceiling and several long curls of paint flicked off. "Oopsie. My bad."

"You're in trouble, big time." Zach glanced up. "Aunt Neece isn't going to be happy about what you did."

"I'll tell her you did it, Zach. Threw a rock and hit it, or something." I liked my solution. From the expression on my little brother's face, he didn't so much. I studied the dragon, more impressive and beautiful than any I'd ever painted. Why did I feel the need to protect this creature?

"What I could really go for," said the dragon, clicking its talons together as if it was drumming its fingers, "are some nice hors d'oeuvres."

"Oar derbs?" Zach tried out the strange word. "What's that?"

The dragon laughed, or at least that's what I thought it was. It sounded like a revving engine crossed with a cat's purr, and puffs of noxious steam boiled from its lips and nose.

Zach and I stepped back. I mouth-breathed some more. Zach pinched his nostrils together. Hope that didn't offend the creature.

"Hors d'oeuvres." The dragon settled onto its haunches, curled a slender leathery tail around its legs, and stared down at us. "It's a fancy French word that means..." It tapped one talon on its chin. "Snack. A small meal for when you're a wee bit hungry."

"I've heard that word before, but we don't speak French," I told him. From his deep voice, I guessed this dragon was male. Maybe female dragons had curlier eyelashes. I noted the folds of skin around his eyes. Nope, no eyelashes at all.

"Yeah, only American," Zach added.

"That's English, Zach. We *speak* English. We *are* American."

Zach gave me the roll-eyes. Mama hates it when Zach does that to her, but I don't mind. I ignore it, mostly. Or give it back.

"I speak French, Italian, Spanish, Mandarin, Latin..." The dragon ticked off a tally using his digits. For a second, he reminded me of Aunt Neece. "And a few ancient languages that no one uses anymore. Plus the clan lingos."

"Clan lingos?" I asked.

"Dragon-speak. The same for all color clans, with a tiny difference here and there, and there and here."

"Wow," I said. Questions crowded my head. Who knew dragons were so smart? Dragons come in different colors? And all of them can talk? I considered telling him about counting in his head instead of on his fingers, um, claws, but decided not to. He could be using his talons for emphasis, like Aunt Neece does.

"But back to those hors d'oeuvres..." The dragon lifted one spiked eyebrow. "Got any fish? Maybe some canned sardines?"

Zach and I exchanged glances. The only kind of fish Zach liked, and the only one Aunt Neece had, I didn't think dragons would go for.

"We have sushi." I waited, hoping to hear the engine/cat purr sound again.

"Excellent!"

His hot breath washed over me. My nose stung. Remember to mouth-breathe, Aidan! Easy to believe he liked fish.

"California rolls? Lobster rolls? What?" He rubbed his front claws together. The purr cranked up. More smoke piped from his nose. Small wonder that Aunt Neece's fire alarm didn't go off. And why wasn't she jumping up to come check out the commotion in her sunroom? Probably still watching Her Show from behind her closed eyelids. Daddy watched baseball the same way.

Zach turned and jetted off toward the kitchen before I had a chance to stop him. I flashed the dragon a sheepish grin and inched a little farther away. The stench surrounded him like a cloud. In a moment, Zach returned with two plastic trays filled with sushi. "No lobster rolls, but we have crab and shrimp."

"Purrr-fect," the dragon rumbled. He lowered his head to our level and gave the smile again. For a dragon, he sure had white teeth, even with his awful breath.

I helped my little brother open the package. Drawn by the scent of food, Aunt Neece's gray tabby cat, Mr. Pig, ambled into the sunroom. Zach and I froze. Did dragons eat cats? If Mr. Pig had been the dragon's size, I might have wondered if he might eat dragon meat. Mr. Pig weighed twenty pounds and had never met a food bowl he didn't like.

Mr. Pig stared at the dragon. I held my breath. Then something unexpected happened. Mr. Pig trilled, the dragon replied in a low rumble, and that fat cat sauntered over and walked lazy circles around the dragon, rubbing the sides of his mouth here and there. Aunt Neece called that "marking behavior" and it meant Mr. Pig considered the dragon part of his family.

My aunt's other cat—a delicate old black and white female named Sissy—probably still cowered beneath Aunt Neece's bed. Zach always picked her up and kissed her all over her head. She didn't like it much and took off like she'd been flung from a slingshot as soon as we walked in the door. No worries about Sissy hanging out with our scaly guest.

The dragon turned his attention from Mr. Pig back to the sushi.

I managed to find my voice. It had frozen in my throat when I thought the dragon might turn Mr. Pig into one giant California cat roll. "Do you want soy sauce with that?"

The dragon bobbed his head. A line of greenish drool slipped from one corner of his mouth and dropped onto the area rug, where it singed a circle. How would I explain *that* to Aunt Neece? A huge dragon slobbered volcanic drool on your rug. Right.

"I'll take a pinch of that pickled ginger and just a smidge of wasabi, if you please." The dragon lowered his body and hunkered down, bringing his head to our level. Good thing. My neck had a cramp from looking up. He waited patiently while Zach opened the soy sauce packet. I tore off a strip of the ginger and dabbed wasabi onto several pieces of California roll.

My shoulders relaxed. "Wasabi's way too spicy hot for me. Tried it once and it burned all the way down my throat." I crinkled my nose.

"Not a problem for me. I'm used to a little fire in my head," the dragon said.

Zach shot me a look and I knew what he was thinking. How do you serve sushi to a dragon? I shrugged, put three rolls into the palm of my hand, careful to hold my fingers flat and out of the way, then took a steadying breath. If it worked when I fed sugar cubes to my friend Olivia's horse, maybe it would work for dragons.

When I extended my sushi-loaded hand toward him, the dragon used the tips of his talons to stab one roll at a time. After he had all three on his purplish pointy tongue, he closed his mouth. I pulled back my hand, amazed that he hadn't touched my skin. I checked for scorch marks all the same.

His eyes closed. Rumbles sounded from his throat, a dragon form of *yum*, I guessed. Then his eyes popped open. "Oh no." He flung his front legs wide. "Seek cover!"

I grabbed Zach by the shirtsleeve and yanked. We dove behind the rockers and covered our heads. The dragon's nose rippled three times then a whoosh of air flew out, sounding like a dog squeeze-toy whistle. I peeked from behind the rockers. Sizzling green blobs clung to one wall and the paint dissolved and dripped to the floor in long beige streaks.

"Oopsie." The dragon snuffled. "Wasabi gives me the *sneeze-uls* every time." He pronounced the word like *measles*, only with a *sn* in front.

Zach lunged from his hidey-hole. "You didn't do it right."

The dragon lowered his bulky head and stared eye-to-eye at my brother.

"You're supposed to do it like this." Zach put his nose into the crook of his arm and faked a sneeze. I had taught him that. Imagine him listening—and having the nerve to teach it to a dragon.

The dragon raised a front leg and mimicked the correct sneeze position, then looked to Zach for approval.

"Perfect!"

"Why should I *sneeze-ul* all over myself? Doesn't make sense."

I took over. "When you sneeze—um, sneeze-ul— into your elbow, you don't blow junk all over the place." My gaze flicked to the slime dissolving Aunt Neece's wall paint. "Used to be, people sneezed into their hands, but then they'd touch stuff and spread germs really bad. Now, we do it this way." I didn't add: and your arm scales can handle dragon nose goop way better than Aunt Neece's sunroom.

The dragon took two more pieces of sushi, this time without wasabi. Suppose he didn't want to sneeze-ul into his arm. He closed his eyes and swooned with pleasure.

"What's your name?" Zach asked. That was my brother. He had to know everything. But it kept me from having to ask.

The dragon opened his eyes and glanced up to the ruined patch on the ceiling and the streaks on the wall, then back down toward Zach. "Just call me *J*. The last time I spoke my real name inside a building, it wasn't pretty."

"Why?" My brother and his need to know. But, I was curious too.

"Dragon-speak is nothing like human-speak. It comes out all fire and heat, and you wouldn't understand it besides. We only speak it to each other."

"Okay then. J is fine," I said quickly. The ceiling and wall and the melted place on the rug would be enough to explain to Aunt Neece. If J set the sunroom afire, Zach and I would never be invited back.

Kicked out of Camp Neece for good.

Only, I didn't want to get kicked out.

This place was getting interesting.

CHAPTER THREE

Three containers of sushi, twelve raw hot dogs, two bags of corn chips, a box of Swiss cakes, a six-pack of cola, cinnamon rolls, and a bag of gummy bears: all gone. Aunt Neece would have to go to the store again. That would not put her in her happy place. I cleaned up the wrappers and cans, and brushed up the chocolate crumbs and flecks of sugar.

"Got any games?" J sat back and belched, twice.

I crinkled my nose and tried not to gag. The smell was atrocious, but years of babysitting and changing dirty diapers had steeled me against stench, a little. Even Mr. Pig squinted and flattened back his whiskers. J hadn't burned any more slobber spots on the rug, but his table manners needed work.

"I have video games." Zach stood and did his wiggle-butt dance.

"No can do," J said. "The dragon is always the bad guy! Plus electronics mess with my mind."

"Mine too." I was getting to like J, a lot. With him close—stink and all—I felt safer from dark things.

Zach shot me a look. "Aunt Neece has puzzles, I think." Like he could sit still long enough to put together one of Aunt Neece's hard-beyond-belief, gazillion-piece puzzles. Mama said she thought that puzzle Aunt Neece had spread out on the dining room table was the same one from when *she* was twelve.

"Nah. No puzzles." J wiggled his talons. "I find them difficult to handle, and I'm not very patient. When a piece doesn't fit, I turn it to ash. Anger issues." He screwed up his lips. "Oh!" He motioned to the box. "You have a deck of cards."

"They're yours, aren't they? They were in *your* box." I shook my head. What would I tell my friends at school? What did you do on summer vacation, Aidan? *Oh, I went to Camp Neece, where I ate sushi and played cards with a dragon.*

"I only know Go Fish and Slap Jack," Zach said. I had learned Spades and Hearts from Aunt Neece, but the past few times I'd seen her, she didn't seem interested in playing.

"Oh, let's play Go Fish. I do *so* love fish." J winked one green eye.

The deck looked ordinary enough when Zach took it from the Rainy Day Box. A movement snatched my attention. I glanced toward the window. An ebony, spine-studded face glared at me through the glass, same as the shadowy shape from the storm cloud, only this one was solid, as real as the green dragon sitting on the sunroom rug. Its face wasn't goofy or kind like J's—instead, it stared as if it would delight in slaughtering all three of us.

J swiveled, following my line of vision. A low growl rumbled his throat. The green dragon and I exchanged looks. When I turned back to face the window, the ebony dragon had vanished. J shifted to settle closer to me. Across from us, Zach shuffled, dealt out seven cards apiece, then sat back to study his hand, oblivious to the dragon at the window. An unspoken knowing passed between me and the green dragon. Now was not the time to make a ruckus.

I picked up my cards and acted as normal as possible, willing my pulse to calm. "If you can't handle puzzle pieces, how can you handle—" I stopped when I saw J's cards, five times the size of ours, fanned out in one claw.

J looked up. "Beg your pardon?"

"Nothing." So what if the cards did strange things? I was playing with a green dragon that used to fit in the palm of my hand, and was made from stone and wasn't even alive besides, not to mention the rock and sword, or that dark dragon.

"You don't have any anger issues with Go Fish too, do you?" I asked.

J's eyes peeped over the edge of his cards like twin neon marbles, the triangular pupils constricted to thin lines. "Only when I lose."

"Any threes?" Zach asked. I handed over a three of hearts. J shook his head. "Do you really stay in that box, like, most of the time?" my brother asked.

"Beats the street." J straightened his cards. "Been my home for the last eight hundred years. But before that... well, let's just say, I haven't always been a morph."

"Eight hundred years? Jeez. You're old." Zach stared at J over his hand of cards. "Got any tens?"

J and I both said, "Go fish."

"What's a morph?" I kept my voice calm. Act like everything is normal and it is, Aidan.

"A morph is a dragon hiding in a figure. Most are made from stone, but not always," J said. "Any kings?" Zach and I gave one card each. Smoke leaked from the corners of his smile. "How about twos?"

"Go fish!" Zach and I said.

J drew from the deck, nestled his latest card into his claw, and looked up. "Actually, I'm only a smidge over eleven."

Zach snorted. "No way."

"Yes, way," J parroted back in a sing-song fashion. "Dragons only celebrate birthdays every hundred and fifty human years. Long time to wait, in your terms, but our parties are huge and the cake is immense." He did that rumble dragon laugh again. "Been larger fun since the Dark Ages. More traditions, bigger reunions." He pursed his lips, a comical expression for a dragon. "We do have a harder time hiding nowadays, though, what with humans infesting every corner of the globe. No offense to you two. We now have our own place to party. A separate place from here. You might say we were driven out."

J plucked at his beard. "We don't stick candles on top of the cakes. Had to cut that out, in the nineteenth century. Last time we used candles, the resulting fire nearly wiped out a village in Guiana. Not pretty. And that whole blowing out the flames thing that's part of your tradition? Not a good idea either. Dragon breath fries the sugar icing. Turns the whole cake into one smoldering black blob."

Zach and I listened, nodding at the right times, like we talked about dragon birthday parties and the Dark Ages and charred cake every day. J's banter further calmed my jitters. Better for me to act like this whole thing didn't faze me, or Zach would blab to Aunt Neece. She'd think I was having some sort of mental breakdown and tell my parents. Nope, I had to keep it together.

"Are there more dragons besides you? And if so, where are they?" My little brother, the information gathering guy. Go, Zach. Exactly what I wanted to know.

J looked from the sunroom windows. The sky was pewter gray and heavy with clouds. "Of course. Hundreds and hundreds of us. Thousands and thousands even."

Zach slumped forward in shock. I tapped his hand so he'd tilt up his cards. Like I cared if he lost, but really, what fun is Go Fish if you know what your opponent holds?

"So where are they, all these dragons?" I leaned toward J. "I've never seen one." I tried for an amused tone, but it came out full of yearning. I could do without ever seeing that dark dragon again, but others? Heck yeah.

Mr. Pig had curled up beside J. The dragon trailed one talon in loops around the cat's ears. Mr. Pig vibrated with pleased purrs. "Ever hear the term 'hidden in plain sight'?" J asked.

"Of course," I said. "I hide things in my paintings all the time."

Zach shook his head. How he could say *no* amazed me, what with all the other teachable moments we had endured at Camp Neece. For sure, Aunt Neece had covered the subject.

"Let me give you an example." J directed his gaze outside again, to one of the elephant ear leaves. "See that lizard?"

We followed his pointing talon. "Yes."

The little lizards, green anoles, were so plentiful and ordinary, they blended into the background. They turned from new-leaf green to muddy brown, depending on where they rested. Nature's camouflage, Aunt Neece called it.

"Nine out of ten lizards are dragons," J said. "We call them *dainties*. If you look closely, you can see the dents on their sides where they store their wings."

Yes! I'd seen the dent and the wings! Was that the deal with the little lizard I saw earlier? The threat was the only thing I had invented, that first time.

J studied me for a moment, then nodded. Like he knew what I was thinking.

"Masters of disguise, those dainties," J continued. "Same with dragonflies. A dragonfly is a different kind of dainty that chooses to flaunt its wings. Quite ostentatious if you ask me."

"Os-ten-what?" Zach asked.

"Ostentatious," J replied in a teachy sort of voice. "Means being overly showy."

"Get real," Zach said. "Dragonflies are dragons? What a load of phooey."

But the idea thrilled me. I thought of the darting dragonflies I saw every day, dipping and zipping above the grass. As if they were drawn in by the car exhaust, they appeared everywhere, even in Tallahassee and Lake City, even in the middle of town. My drawing pad contained page after page of dragonflies and damselflies. And to think, dragons in disguise had really surrounded me all along!

J twisted his mouth to one side. Swiss cake crumbs tumbled to the floor like chocolate hail. "You're talking to a dragon—a *morph*, by the way—who turned from a piece of jade into this." He swished one giant clawed front foot down his body like a game show host presenting a new car. "Belicve me, or not. Your choice. No scales off my tail."

"Are damselflies dainties too?" I asked.

J tilted his head, studying me with new interest—maybe even a little respect. "You know the difference?"

"Dragonflies keep their wings straight out to the side. Damselflies either spread their wings a little or fold them back behind them when they land."

Because of my mom, I knew more about the little air dancers than most people. Fanciful creatures with names like common green darner and my favorite, the comet darner, the only Southern dragonfly with red markings.

"Dragonflies and damselflies are sometimes called *odes*. That's slang for members of the insect order *Odonata*." I set my cards face-down and warmed up to the subject. "You have to be careful when you handle one. Have to grasp it from below, like this." I mimed the finger position with one hand. "If you damage its wings, it can't fly and feed itself. Then it will die."

"Aidan and Mama tramp around the swamp catching bugs in nets." Zach pulled his dull face. "Mama says Aidan is like a magnet for those bugs."

I ignored him. "I use a field guide and magnifying lens to check the markings and colors. After I snap a quick picture, I release them. The photos help me to make charcoal and pastel sketches for my collection."

"Only dragonflies are dainties, but not *all* dragonflies are dainties," J said. "Damselflies are exactly as they seem, no more no less."

Unbelievable. One of those sleepy mid-mornings, when Mama woke me at dawn to slog around some pond, creek bed, or riverbank, I had probably held a dragon in my hands. "How can I tell which ones are dainties?"

J picked up another Swiss cake and popped it into his mouth. "Afraid you can't. You humans look but do not see. Only other dragons can detect the subtle markings."

"Where else do they live? Where, where, where?" Zach bounced.

I shot my brother a slit-eyed look. The whole three-word thing was making me crazoid.

"Near the cool Florida springs. Near the lakes and rivers and streams. In the deep woods, in the city parks, in your dreams." J waved his claw in loopy circles. "Everywhere you find a place, you'll find an incognito dragon." J leaned down and widened his eyes until they were the size of moon pies—and I thought my brother was the only drama king.

J took a noisy swig of soda and let out a wet burp. Smelled like something had crawled inside that dragon and died. Zach held his nose clamped shut with two fingers. I blinked the burning mist from my eyes and mouth-breathed. Mr. Pig jerked from his nap and sneezed.

"Kiddos!" Aunt Neece called out.

Oh no. My eyes darted to Zach's. His were perfect circles. We both looked at J. Chocolate from the ten Swiss cakes smeared the wiry fuzz beneath his lower jaw. He burped again. Soft drinks and dragons didn't mix. A smell like rotten eggs baking in the sun hung in the air.

"What do you two want for dinner?" Aunt Neece stood at the door to the sunroom.

"I... I..." My mouth refused to work with my brain. Zach sat there like a lump. For once, my little brother kept quiet. Good thing we'd cleaned up the trash and soft drink cans.

When I tore my eyes from Aunt Neece and swung around to see how J would handle this situation, he had vanished. His cards, a normal size now, fanned out on the carpet, luckily hiding the slobber spot. Maybe if we could distract her, Aunt Neece wouldn't notice the polka-dot wall or the turned-over fern and rearranged furniture. Oh, and the curling paint overhead. Don't forget that.

"Thought I bought hot dogs, but I can't seem to find them anywhere." Aunt Neece scratched her head. Her stick-up red hair stood up even more.

Didn't she smell the dragon burp? How could she *not* smell the dragon burp?

Her nose wasn't working but she noticed the extra playing cards. "A little old for an imaginary friend, aren't you?"

A slight smile lifted the corners of her lips and her right hand fingers sought the silver ring on her left hand, twirling it around and around. She turned her head toward the cedar chest, to the Rainy Day Box. For an instant, her face changed. None of those tiny wrinkles she called crows' feet creased the skin around her eyes. Her skin lifted and a pink color bloomed on her cheeks. My Aunt Neece looked much younger, my age even. Then I blinked, and she had shifted back, my regular ole aunt again. Just like what had happened earlier with the lizard turned dragon.

Zach threw down his cards and jumped up. "Pizza, pizza, pizza!"

"I suppose we can call for delivery." Aunt Neece turned and headed for the kitchen, trailed by Zach. Mr. Pig trotted behind them. If that fat cat had fingers, he would dial out for food himself.

No doubt the pizza would be pepperoni and sausage, extra cheese for my aunt. Zach would spit out onions and peppers or any odd topping. I'd seen him launch a black olive halfway across the room. I could hear them in the kitchen, talking about food and how trying new things was good, with Mr. Pig commenting in exaggerated yowls. Aunt Neece and another one of her teachable moments. She might as well save her breath.

I picked up the box, took out the tiny green dragon figurine and held it in my cupped hand. I turned it one way, then the other, squinting to study it as close as possible. How did the magic work, and why had J changed back when Aunt Neece appeared? What was up with Aunt Neece anyway? Questions hopscotched over each other in my brain.

But the best part? Dragons were real! "I knew it. I knew it. I knew it!" I didn't even care that I'd said it three times like Zach.

"See you later, J," I whispered, running my fingers lightly across the cool jade. I nestled the morph back into the Rainy Day Box and shut the lid.

I tamped down thoughts about any dragon harboring evil.

CHAPTER FOUR

"Hey, slow down and chew!" Aunt Neece scolded. "You're both eating like someone's going to snatch that pizza away from you."

I looked up from my plate at Zach. Tomato sauce smeared his lips and one dollop had dripped onto his T-shirt. "Gah, you are such a pig."

"Mama says if it's good enough to eat, then it's good enough to wear," my brother fired back.

Aunt Neece pointed to a sliver of pepperoni attached to my shirt by a shred of mozzarella. "You have no room to fuss at him, missy. Since your mama has the same affliction, it must be a family trait." She looked down to her own clothing, at a splatter of sauce beneath the first button. "Mercy me."

All of the scold-energy drained from my aunt and her face yielded to one of her throaty laughs. Zach and I joined in. As we wound down to a few hiccupped chuckles, I slipped bits of cheese and sausage to Mr. Pig, the real porker of the group. He purred and gnawed, casting cat love-eyes my way.

I looked from the kitchen nook window. Though the darkening sky still held a threat, the drizzle had stopped. I longed to see J, to get back to that box. Drat. Instead, I helped Aunt Neece and Zach clear the table and wash up the few dishes.

For the rest of the afternoon, Zach and I watched television, argued over controlling the remote, and drove Aunt Neece nutso. A couple of times, Zach leaned over to whisper something about the dragon and I jabbed him into silence.

"I'm hungry," Zach announced after a while. He popped to his feet and aimed for the refrigerator.

"Stop." Aunt Neece lowered the sound on the flat screen. "You know the rule. Kitchen closed an hour ago."

"Shoot." Zach flopped down.

Good thing Zach had said the right word. Mama and Daddy had been none too happy when he brought that Other Bad Word home and tried it on for size. Zach lost privileges—all his games and laptop—for three weeks. One day he'd learn to be creative, like me. I said *sugar* when things made me nutso. I was sure cursing wouldn't cut it at Camp Neece either.

"Aidan, please go brush your teeth." Aunt Neece pointed in the direction of the bathroom. "Bed is in half an hour. Tomorrow after breakfast, we're touring the Capitol."

"Geez, she's crabbity," I mumbled when I was far enough down the hall Aunt Neece couldn't hear. She usually let us stay up until we fell asleep in front of the TV.

I brushed and flossed, and picked out about a pound of junk from between my braces. I'd have to tell Mama later, how I think I saved an entire slice in there—she always called every night when we were away from home, to say hello and find out about our day. It was either that, or tell her about J. I let out a laugh and a dollop of toothpaste foam flew from my lips and landed on the mirror. Woops. I wiped it clean with a washcloth.

I wasn't full-on excited about going downtown to the Capitol. I had seen the view from the twenty-second floor on a field trip in fourth grade, but Zach had never visited the official state buildings in Tallahassee. Rather stay here and wait for the rain to start again... and what would happen if we opened the box when it wasn't raining?

The dragon popped into my mind, his big green smelly self. I tried Zach's repeat-o-matic trick. "I hope, hope, hope it will storm."

I grimaced at my reflection, drawing my lips back and moving my head to the right then to the left, checking for pizza crud I might have missed. Mirrors always enchanted me. Not that I am stuck-up and all into gazing at myself. Mirrors seemed magical. If I could figure a way to breach the silver force field, I might step into another world where things looked the same, but different. A place where most anything could happen.

A loud rap sounded behind me. I pitched the toothbrush into its holder and snatched open the door. "Jeez, Zach. Can't a person have some privacy for even one hot second?"

I leaned out, searching the hallway in both directions, but Zach wasn't there. The hall was empty, yet my nose picked up the trace of decay. In the distance, I heard my aunt and brother's voices mingled with the television's low drone.

Someone, or some*thing*, had been there.

Aunt Neece flipped the overhead light on and off, on and off, on and off.

"Sugar," I mumbled. "Morning already?" I groaned and dug my face into the pillow. It had taken me forever to fall asleep. Every sound had freaked me out.

"It's eight-thirty, kiddos. Time to get up and have breakfast."

If I had my way most days, I'd sleep until noon. So would Zach. In two weeks, we'd have to be up by five-thirty. Ugh.

When neither of us made a move in a few minutes, the lights flickered again, on and off, on and off. "If we want to see anything downtown, we'd best get a move on. Rains every afternoon, this time of year."

Rain? Okay, so that was a glimmer of hope I would see J again, anything to get my mind focused on happier things. "Better get up, Zach. She'll start blasting that old stereo if we don't." And she would, too. Where Aunt Neece had found a CD with marching band music, I didn't know. She would turn it up so loud, I'd think the entire FSU Marching Chiefs had tromped into the bedroom, enough to scare the beejeebies out of me.

I stopped by the bathroom long enough to rake a comb through my hair and splash water on my face, then followed Zach into the kitchen. Aunt Neece stood at the stove, flipping her special confetti pancakes. She always added rainbow sugar sprinkles into the batter to entice Zach. I'm older and I made sure not to act all excited, but I liked those speckled pancakes too. Would J like them? Perhaps if we added some ground-up trout? Oh yuck.

"Want to finish up this last batch?" Aunt Neece asked me.

Of course I did! I nodded and grinned. I loved cooking with my aunt, had done it since I could barely reach the counter. I'd even mastered a few of her recipes good enough to make back home. By myself!

I scrubbed my hands again and took spatula duty. She dipped batter and I watched for the tiny air bubbles to pop to the surface as the pancakes cooked. Ready? Nope, a little more. Okay, flip!

"Good job, baby. You've really gotten the hang of it."

Her praise warmed up my heart. Zach stood next to me, angling for the spatula. "No go, Zach. This is *my* deal."

Sissy slunk through the kitchen and hunkered down next to her empty food bowl. Mr. Pig sat by his, licking his lips and paws. Aunt Neece divided the stack of browned pancakes onto plates and herded Zach and me to the table.

"My poor old gal." She leaned down and ran her hand down Sissy's back. "You don't have a chance to eat with Mr. Pig pushing you aside." She spooned an extra dollop of cat food into Sissy's bowl, then distracted Mr. Pig with a couple of kitty treats.

As usual, we ate at the oak table in the country kitchen. I loved the kitchen, with its bright white walls, tall windows, and lemon yellow curtains. Much better than the dining room. That table was dark wood and the room around it felt stuffy. Besides, one end was always taken up with a puzzle spread all over. Then there was the sunroom. No way. If I looked up and saw a demon dragon watching me eat...

"Put butter between those pancakes while they're hot," Aunt Neece said, then she went back to retrieve the small pottery pitcher of sugar cane syrup she had warmed in the microwave.

We both drank milk, though Zach wanted soda. Camp Neece rule: No soda for breakfast. Only milk or fruit juice. Period.

I snuck glances toward the Rainy Day Box, sitting there on the cedar chest. What if J could come with us today? I could get in huge trouble if he changed into his real self and crashed into anything, or sneezed on something worth a boatload of money. But my pocket would be safe as any old wooden box, and he was just a carved morph after all. I decided *yes*. I wanted J with me, always.

An hour later, Aunt Neece negotiated Tallahassee traffic. Her cell phone sang from its mount on the dash. She slowed and pulled into a parking lot to answer. No talking on cell phones or texting while driving, a rigid Neece rule.

"Your brain can't handle two things at once and do them both well," she said, rolling into a space at a 7-Eleven. "You can kill your fool self and take some poor innocent person with you."

Aunt Neece put the call on speakerphone. A bubbly woman's voice sang out, one of those voices that makes music. "Guess what? I managed to get permission for the kids to visit the governor's office."

After a few minutes, Aunt Neece said goodbye to the caller, then pressed the off button. Both hands on the wheel, and full attention to the road. "Hear that? My friend Miz Bridie has yanked some strings for us. Not everyone gets to go into the governor's private office."

Zach spotted a tall building shaped like a soda can. "Is that the Capitol?"

Aunt Neece and I laughed. I felt a little bad for Zach since he didn't know better.

"No, honey. That's a hotel. Used to be the Round Holiday Inn when it was first built. Another company owns it now."

"It's still round," he mumbled.

She motioned out the windshield. "You can't see the Capitol yet, but if you keep looking, you might catch a glimpse soon. It's much taller."

Zach wiggled. "And we get to go all the way to the top?"

"Yep. Sure do. Up twenty-two floors. But we're meeting Miz Bridie first."

We parked at a place called Kleman Plaza and walked two blocks. J's morph bumped against my thigh, nestled in one pocket of my cargo shorts. With every step, it vibrated. *No, J. You can't come out here!* I stared up at the dark clouds gathering in the distance. Had I made a mistake?

At the top of a series of concrete steps, a long fountain spread out at the base of a skyscraper. Waterfalls dropped from the upper level into a blue pool filled with statues of leaping dolphins. Aunt Neece took out her smartphone and made us pull a cheesy pose. Experience told me there would be a lot of posing during our Camp Neece stay.

Two officers stood in the entranceway. Since Zach and I had flown before, we knew about security drills. Put your stuff on the little moving thingy so it could go through an x-ray machine, then wait until the guard motioned for you to step through the detector arch. Zach shelled out two twigs and a dead, dried-up frog from one shorts pocket, then patted the other one and took out four quarters and an unwrapped stick of fuzzy gum. The guards chuckled. He bounded through the arch and didn't set off any alarms. Guess he remembered to leave his folding pocketknife at the house like Aunt Neece asked.

I slid my hand into my pocket and there was J. My chest constricted. Hadn't thought about this when I put the morph in there. I emptied the lip balm, crumpled tissues, and my folding brush. If I showed J's morph, I was *so* busted. Sugar! What to do?

I left it there, took a deep breath to settle my jangly nerves, stepped through the arch. My stomach roiled. The guard waved me past. Was it because the figure wasn't metal or was it shielded by magic? The breath puffed from me in a relieved whoosh.

My brother asked one of the guards about a million and one questions. Perfect distraction, in case the officer might notice the rocky lump in my pocket. The man was a good sport, and he motioned us toward the lobby.

"Kids, that's my friend Miz Bridie," Aunt Neece said, nodding toward the woman waiting by the elevators.

Miz Bridie was dressed in a plain black skirt and jacket. A patchwork shirt in wild colors peeked from beneath the business suit, like a rainbow shining between storm clouds. She walked with a little sway and used a neat cane. The top curved into a sleek bird's head with a ruby eye on either side.

"Glad you all could come today," Miz Bridie called out. She had twinkly blue eyes and reddish hair a little darker than Aunt Neece's. Her whole face got involved in her smile. I liked her instantly.

She gave Aunt Neece a hug and turned to Zach and me. "I've heard about you two. So glad to finally get to meet you! Let's go to the governor's office first, then we'll take a look from the top." She stepped into the elevator, we climbed aboard, and she pressed a button. "Hold on now! This elevator hauls boogie!"

Why did I feel as if we could end up most anywhere, somewhere magical? As if she read my thoughts, Miz Bridie winked. She fired off questions—What have you painted lately, Aidan? How's your baseball career going, Zach? Clearly, she already knew a lot about us.

"Sometimes, when I step into this elevator, I feel like it will pop from the top of the building and lift off into space." Miz Bridie butterflied one hand in the air, tracing a path up and up. "Pass Mars and Saturn! Go through a black hole and end up in an Otherworld with creatures not seen on Earth."

Zach jiggled in place. "Cool!"

Aunt Neece cleared her throat and gave Miz Bridie a stern look. Miz Bridie chuckled.

"You must be very quiet when we go into the private office area," Miz Bridie said when the doors whooshed open. "Folks think they're doing important work in there." She nodded to another security officer behind a desk and he pressed a button to allow us to enter a set of tall, carved wooden doors.

I paused in front of a long gilded mirror. The others walked ahead a few steps while I checked my reflection and smoothed a flip-up curl. Dark smoke rose behind me. It wove around my head like a pair of webbed wings. The scent of something nasty stung my nose.

A low growl sounded from my pocket. The morph vibrated. I pulled it out. J sprung to his full height, snarling at the dark figure in the mirror.

"No! Change back! Change back!" I strained to keep my voice low, yet urgent. J looked away from the mirror, crimped his eyebrows together, then poofed back into my pocket. Just in time.

Aunt Neece looked over her shoulder and motioned for me.

One last glance—no smoke, no dragon, just me in the fancy mirror, and my hair was doing that bad-flip thing again. I jogged to catch up. Secure in my pocket, J's morph bounced against my upper thigh; my protector moved with me.

A long hallway led to the office of the lieutenant governor—the second in command to the governor himself. We peeked in for a moment before continuing to the last door. The governor's assistant met us and led us inside. Another long mirror hung above a table. I moved as far from it as possible in case something dark loomed on the other side, just out of sight.

"Lookit!" Zach pointed to the huge flat screen television mounted on one wall. Leave it to my brother to zero in on the electronics. I walked around, noticing the collection of shiny vintage security badges and photographs. Zach took in the sports memorabilia and said wow a few more times.

"Would you like your pictures taken sitting behind his desk?" Miz Bridie asked.

Even Aunt Neece's eyes widened. We took turns posing, then the assistant took a picture of all three of us.

"I'll be the governor one day," Zach announced.

"Or I will," I said, not too worried I'd have competition from my brother, since his real goal when not at the Capitol was to be a huge, big league baseball star with a fancy car and gobs of money.

"Let's go on up to the top." Aunt Neece stored her smartphone in her jacket pocket. We thanked the governor's assistant. I kept my face pointed straight forward when we passed the mirror on the way to the secured doors.

The express elevator took us up so fast, my ears popped. Zach launched onto the observation deck as soon as the doors parted on the twenty-second floor. All of Tallahassee spread out around us.

Zach ran from one window to the next, pointing to different buildings. "What's that over there? And that one? And *that* one?"

Miz Bridie named a few: Florida State University and Doak Campbell Stadium, Leon High School, and Florida A & M University.

"Some days, when it's clear, you can see all the way to the coast." Miz Bridie tipped her head toward one section of the landscape where the trees dominated. A wall of purple clouds roiled in the distance. "Those deep, dark woods are where all kinds of magical things live."

Couldn't she tell how old we were, well, *I* was? She acted like we were little kids. Then Zach, who was really still sort of a little kid, asked, "What kind of things?"

Miz Bridie glanced toward Aunt Neece, then winked down at us. "That's a story for another day."

Wait—what? The way she looked at Aunt Neece, the way she said that, made me really, really, *really* want to hear that story.

Miz Bridie ambled toward the elevators. "You can stop by and see my little office, if you'd like," she called over her shoulder. "It's a bit... unusual."

We descended a few floors and followed her, quiet again. Whoever these important people were, they sure didn't like noise. Miz Bridie's office faced south, she told us, with a good view of those enchanted woods. Stepping inside, I saw flamingos and fanciful colored things everywhere—lamps, statues, pillows. She had an L-shaped desk, but beyond that and a computer, the room didn't look all stiff, like you couldn't touch anything. I sat on one of the two cushy chairs. Zach wandered around the room, fingering all the bright gewgaws.

One figurine caught my attention. I glanced from it to Miz Bridie. "Is that... a dragon?"

"Uh-hum." She tilted her head. When she smiled, the skin around her bright eyes crinkled.

"May I pick it up?"

"Yes, but *don't* take off the little blind across the eyes." She held up a finger. "Very important."

Aunt Neece fiddled with her ring, twirling it around and around. Then she launched into some discussion about their writing group. “You wouldn’t believe what Jolene did with that Jasper character of hers. Simply scandalous.”

My aunt told some detailed back and forth story about the Jolene person, flicking her eyes at me off and on like she was worried I’d break something I guess. I tuned out their totally boring conversation and lifted the figure from its deep blue, velvet-lined box. Why wasn’t it closed up? Not a morph, I guessed. Still, pretty. The dragon was larger than the one in my pocket and carved from cocoa-brown wood. Rows of pointed scales lined the body, tail and head, and a long beard curled beneath its chin. I wanted to check out its eyes, but the thin strip of cloth covered that part of its head.

Zach whispered in my ear, “Looks like J, except brown.”

Miz Bridie, still deep in conversation with Aunt Neece, glanced our way and winked. I snugged the figurine back into its nest.

We posed for another picture, this one with our host, on a couch she told us had “once lived in the governor’s mansion,” then Aunt Neece led the way out. At the elevator doors, Miz Bridie gave us pillowy hugs. Zach leapt into the elevator—he never stepped on like a normal person—and Aunt Neece followed.

Miz Bridie gave me another quick hug after I thanked her for everything. “Did you enjoy your visit?” she asked.

“Yes ma’am. I—”

Her russet eyebrows lifted. I decided to be bold. “Do you believe in dragons—like *real* dragons?”

She lowered her voice. “Why, yes. I do.”

“Your dragon is beautiful,” I whispered back.

When she smiled, my heart felt all warm.

"Thank you, Aidan. I'll be sure to tell K."

The saliva dried up in my mouth. Miz Bridie chuckled.

Aunt Neece placed her finger on the button to keep the elevator doors open and tapped her foot, an impatient rhythm. Zach looked at her, then propped his hands on his hips. Was I holding up the world, seriously? It wasn't like Aunt Neece to be all rushed like she couldn't wait to get us out of here to the Old Capitol, that two-story building in front of the skyscraper.

Miz Bridie glanced toward them, then back to me. She flashed a grin and wink combo, then leaned down and whispered in my ear, "Loving dragons isn't for the weak of spirit. Oh no."

CHAPTER FIVE

After touring the Old Capitol, we stopped for burgers, then by the grocery store. Again.

"Let's make this quick. My radar app shows we're between squall lines. You and Zach pick out some apples and whatever salad greens you want, oh, and bananas." Aunt Neece tapped the notepad in her right hand with the pen in her left. "You shop with your mama, Aidan, so I trust you to select wisely. The bananas—not too ripe, a little green on them."

I held up a stop-hand. "I got this. Really."

"Zach." She pinned my brother with a stern look. "Stay with your sister. Don't make us chase you down across this store." Then back to me, "I'll pick up the few items on my short list and meet you in the bakery in seven minutes, tops."

Zach snapped to full military attention and saluted. I waved. Our aunt bustled away. The produce area was deserted, but I could hear other shoppers in the next aisle. I rolled the cart to the counter holding several varieties of apples. Gala, Granny Smith, or Red Delicious? I couldn't pick a favorite. I bagged two of each. When I turned to lay eyes on my brother, I found him standing at the end cap picking through the bananas.

A thick ebony arm popped from the display. Before I could register the information my eyes sent to my brain, a claw folded around Zach's forearm and tugged.

"Zach!" I closed the space between us so fast, I was barely aware of my feet pounding the hard tile. I grabbed him and pulled, hard.

The claw released and we fell backwards.

Zach rolled off me and popped to his feet. "What the heck? Why'd you tackle me?"

I stood up, brushing my arms and legs. No major scruffs, but the offended skin warned of bruises to come. "It... It... It had you. I—"

"What had me? Nothing but *you*."

"But. It."

"A banana monster?" Zach regarded me with his eyes narrowed. "You are seriously losing it."

Was I? I inched toward the banana display. Except for the two bunches that had landed on the tile, the rest lined up in stacked rows—some green, others close to ripe.

"Just me, kidding around. Okay?" I rescued both bunches of bananas and put them into the cart. "Let's grab some greens and get to the bakery. Aunt Neece doesn't like it when she's on a mission and we make her wait."

Zach lifted both eyebrows and opened his mouth, then shrugged. He jetted off, toward the chilled vertical rows of organic lettuce. I gave the bananas one last glance and followed.

Less than ten minutes later, all three of us raced the bagged groceries to the car, watching the thickening clouds and listening to the low rumble of thunder. J's morph vibrated in my pocket and I sent down a silent plea: *Wait! Please!* My pocket stopped thrumming.

After she steered onto the main street, Aunt Neece glanced my way. "You're sort of quiet, honey. You feeling all right?"

What I wished I could say was *haunted, freaked out*. Instead, I answered, "Sure. I'm good. A little tired is all."

"Looks like we got home in the nick of time," Aunt Neece said when she pulled into the driveway. With Zach busy helping our aunt carry the grocery bags, I slipped J back into his box. A puff of smoke escaped as I shut the lid. Whoa, that was close.

I rejoined the transport team. The second we settled the last bag onto the kitchen counter, Zach dashed toward the stairs. "Hey, where're you going? You're supposed to help me put this stuff up!" I called out.

"Gotta get my pocket knife." His words echoed behind him.

Of course. His stupid folding knife. He carried it everywhere. Probably even slept with the thing.

He appeared minutes later. "About time," I groused. "What took you fifty forevers?"

"It didn't take me that long. Who made you the boss?"

Before I could ramp up the fight, Aunt Neece fired a warning glance. My snark dried up.

I unpacked the nectarines and bananas and piled them into a wire basket on the kitchen counter, just like there wasn't a dragon hanging around in a box in the next room. Zach stacked cans of diced tomatoes and tomato paste in a cabinet by the dishwasher.

Aunt Neece spooled the cash register ticket through her fingers. "Sure hope I got enough kiddo food for you two sponges. You go through groceries like a knife through warm butter."

"Aunt Neece, you say the funniest stuff. Like that about me looking like a plucked rooster after I take a bath and my hair is all wet and sticking out." Zach tore into a bag of chips and crammed a handful into his mouth. "And saying someone is so lazy they won't hit a lick at a snake. What dumb ole person hits snakes with a stick?" He held his arms up, flexed, as if he could wrestle a snake, easy.

"Don't talk with your mouth full, son."

My brother swallowed then rattled on and on. I stared from the kitchen window, past the gingham curtains at the pelting rain. J waited in that box.

Both cats appeared from the back of the house. I popped the seal from the Kitty Treats. Sissy sat back on her haunches and lifted her paws. So sweet. I rewarded her with a snack. Mr. Pig attempted the begging posture, but his belly caused him to list to one side. I gave him a treat. Effort should be rewarded.

"I'm going to rest for a bit before I start dinner," Aunt Neece said. "Think that burger from a couple of hours ago will hold you two a little while?"

"Sure." Zach finger-bumped a box of cereal onto the top shelf of a small pantry. He had to stand on his toes to reach. "And if not, we can have hors d'oeuvres."

Aunt Neece furrowed her eyebrows. "Hors d'oeuvres? Where did you pick up that fancy word?"

I fired the stink-eye at my brother and said, "from the Food Network."

I had lied to my great aunt, and she was one person I *never* lied to. I was no better than a cockroach, and I despised cockroaches. Daddy said every creature served a purpose and I should respect them all. I tried. I even tolerated snakes, at least the non-venomous ones. For my tenth birthday, I got a thick book about Florida snakes. I learned how to tell from their head shapes and colors which ones to avoid. They didn't really freak me out. But cockroaches? Ugh. No use for them. Ditto mosquitoes.

But back to that lie. I stretched things a little sometimes, true. Zach and I did watch the Food Network with Mama, and surely they used that fancy word for a small something to eat when you're just a little hungry. So maybe it wasn't totally a lie.

I vowed to perform some kind of penance, maybe scrub the toilets and sinks in all three of Camp Neece's bathrooms. Lying stains your spirit, Aunt Neece often said. One little lie for three bathrooms? A fair enough trade.

"We watch the Food Network a lot, like *all* the time," I added to make it sound convincing—at least that part was true.

"Ah, I see," Aunt Neece called over her shoulder as she walked toward the living room. Both cats trailed behind her. "Catch the phone if it rings, if you will please. And don't wake me unless some body part is hanging off at a strange angle or bleeding profusely."

"Bleeding?" Zach asked me after she left the room.

I slid a gallon of milk into the refrigerator and tried not to dwell on the new lie staining my spirit. "She's kidding. That's Neece-speak for 'don't mess up my nap unless it's an emergency.'" Aunt Neece napped a lot, but this year more than ever. Was she sick or something?

The storm that made us speed to finish our chores announced its arrival outside. The lights flickered. No problem. If they went out, I knew exactly where the Camp Neece flashlights were stored. The skies turned an angry purple-gray.

Pop! Pop! Pop! We both turned fast. "Wha—what's that noise?" Zach asked. I frowned, then led the way into the sunroom. The wind outside blew sideways, shifting the pelting rain from left to right, then right to left. Something hit the windows, as if bratty bullies stood outside, throwing gravel.

Zach ran to the back glass-paned door. "Look!"

I wiggled in beside him. Round white orbs bounced on the deck like marbles. "What's that? Snow?" He pressed his face to the glass and left an oily print.

"No silly. It hardly ever snows down here, and only in winter." Moisture from my breath condensed on the door glass. "That's hail."

"Think we should wake Aunt Neece?"

"You heard her. Only for bleeding and things hanging at strange angles."

"But she's a weather freak," he insisted.

"Do you see any blood?"

Wind tore at the oak trees in the back yard. Twigs full of green leaves dashed to the ground. In a few minutes, the hail stopped and the bluster settled into smaller gusts tossing the uppermost branches.

Wide porches stretched all the way around the old wooden three-story Victorian house Aunt Neece called a *Painted Lady*, except in the back where she had closed in a section for the sunroom. Unless a hurricane ripped through Tallahassee, the rockers and fern stands remained dry.

The rain rolled in sheeting waves. The pearly chunks of ice melted.

"See? No problem." I looked at Zach. "Know what this means?"

"The Rainy Day Box," we said together.

"I'll get the sushi," Zach said.

"*I'll* make the hors d'oeuvres."

"Like on the Food Channel," Zach said over his shoulder.

"Don't forget to wash your hands." Good thing about being the big sister: I could be the queen when the resident grown-up wasn't awake to interfere. And as the queen, I got the last word. Most times.

A mist twirled from the box as soon as I picked up the morph. The figure shimmered, light flashed, then J stood before us in all of his emerald glory. Wonder swelled up inside me. Nothing beat seeing a dragon in the scaly flesh. Nothing!

"Got a cramp." J looked over his head. He twitched both wings, then folded them by his sides. "Too bad there's no room to stretch." He spotted the sushi and plate of treats and his black slit pupils grew wide. "Oh... may I?"

I backed away from the mini-buffet. J popped six pieces of sushi into his mouth and crammed in two nectarines, pits and all.

"What have you been up to?" the dragon asked. One filmy eyelid slid down and up.

I winked back, quickly so Zach didn't see. "We just got home from downtown, took a tour."

"And we met this funny lady. And we got to sit in the governor's chair!" Zach showed off the Florida surfer-dude twine bracelet. "I got this in the gift shop."

I modeled the new piece of jewelry next to my watch, a mood bracelet that turned different colors depending on how I felt. Right now, it was a deep green-blue. "Means I'm peaceful and calm." I pulled a thin roll of paper from my shorts pocket. "See? It tells me right here in these instructions what color means what."

J pulled on his scruffy chin hairs, cocking his head to listen. Good thing J didn't rat me out to my brother, since his morph had been with us all along. So had a menacing thing that had followed me. I shook off the unease threatening to cramp my stomach.

Instead of soda, I served J filtered ice water. So far, he hadn't belched one time.

Zach fooled with the surfer-dude bracelet, spinning it around and around on his wrist until I wondered if he would wear a rut. "The new Capitol was cool," he said. "But the Old Capitol wasn't as fun."

"It was historic, Zach," I said. Like he'd care. He had dashed from one room to the next, barely taking in the exhibits.

J smacked his rubbery lips. "Do you have any ice cream?" The dragon looked longingly toward the kitchen.

"Sure. Chocolate and vanilla." Zach's face split into a grin. I think he would've fed himself to J if it would've made the dragon happy. Good thing Mr. Pig and Sissy didn't appeal to J, or Zach might have offered the cats on a platter.

"I think..." J tapped his chin. "Vanilla. But with some of those colored sprinkles on top, the kind you had in your pancakes this morning."

My silly brother. Instead of spooning some in a bowl, he brought out the gallon tub and the shaker jar of candy confetti. J grabbed the ice cream, shucked off the lid, and ladled huge frozen chunks into his mouth with his tongue. He motioned for Zach to shake confetti sprinkles into the mix. Halfway through the gallon container, J lifted his head. Colored sprinkles dotted his milky tongue. "Want some?"

Zach and I shook our heads. No way was I eating ice cream á la dragon slobber.

J licked the white melted cream from his lips. "So you don't like history, eh?"

"Some of it," Zach said. "The arrowheads and spear points were cool, and that old gun with the bayonet."

Zach liked old weapons as much as video games. During hunting season, Daddy and his friends hunted to put venison and turkey in our freezer, and he kept those guns locked in a safe. My brother loves the woods as much as I do. We spend a lot of time with Daddy, riding the ATV down narrow unpaved roads, through swamps brimming with mosquitoes and probably our version of Bigfoot, too, if local legends hold any truth. Because Daddy's a fish and game officer, Zach and I know a lot about wildlife: bears, deer, coyotes, bobcats, Florida panthers, not to mention snakes and gators. Daddy taught both of us basic survival skills, something all people that live in the country need to know. How we love to hear our daddy's stories from work.

My brother pulled a face. "That other old museum stuff was boring."

J dropped the empty ice cream container on the floor. Not a single dollop remained—wiped clean, as if it had never held anything. "Oh, I wish you hadn't said that word." J's eyes shifted to the Rainy Day Box.

"What, boring?" Zach jumped around. "It's boring, boring, boring!"

J groaned. The sparkly pink wand rose from the box, spun three times in a circle, and clattered to the tile. Zach and I stepped back. Fog billowed from the wand in curls, a thick vapor that reminded me of when the gardenias by Aunt

Neece's front door bloomed all at once. Too sweet, overpowering. The vapor burned my eyes.

From the fog, an outline appeared. Was it a person? Another creature? The mist cleared and the image took on substance. It was a girl close to my age, but that was where the similarity stopped.

"Did I hear someone say *boring*?" The girl's voice came out high and tinkled like wind chimes. She glanced from me, to Zach, then to the dragon. "J, Whas-sup, dragon-man?"

Both Zach and I had *O*'s for mouths. J took a deep, scale-rippling breath, then frowned and said, "Aidan, Zach, meet Charity."

The girl swung out one arm, then bowed from the waist. "Bemused and demented to meet you."

She stood eye-to-eye with me. Skinny-thin. Dark black hair that looked like she had trimmed it with a pair of garden clippers. Her lips appeared thin and blue around the edges, and her skin was pale as the paper in my favorite sketchpad. I took in her clothing: ripped jeans beaded with dirt; three layers of T-shirts in dingy yellow, orange, and faded black; and cheap purple flip-flops. Each of her toenails was a different color. Around her neck, she wore a necklace made from thick chain with a rhinestone letter C charm. Her ring—a tarnished silver band—pinched tight around the middle finger of her right hand. One earlobe was pierced with pointy studs. Tiny cogs hung from the other, as if a miniature clock had exploded and hit that side of her face.

A Goth-meets-Steampunk look. I liked it, sort of. Radical. Mama would never let me leave the house dressed like that. I'd tried. Closest I came to Steampunk was Grandmother Ivey's old watch, which Charity admired.

"Ooh, can I have it?" Her cool fingers brushed my wrist. I was so surprised, I almost gave it to her. Almost.

I caught a whiff of something unpleasant when she shifted positions—a wet, musty scent blended with hints of other nasty things I couldn't identify.

Except for her odor, I envied Charity a little. No matter how I tried, I could never be wild and bizarre, only plain old Aidan McAllister. Good student. Good daughter. Good everything. I liked myself okay, but sometimes wished to be someone more exciting and interesting.

"D-d-do you live in the box too?" Zach asked.

Charity spit out a sound like a snort and hiss woven together. "In there? You kidding?" She shrugged. "I don't live anywhere."

Mama wouldn't let me get away with the attitude either. It would be nice if I could sashay around and sling such a 'tude. So very cool.

"Charity's homeless," J offered.

"I'm *not*." The girl squared her shoulders and stuck out her chin. "I live wherever and whenever I want."

"Oh, I forget. You always have total control," J mumbled.

When she turned sideways a little, I noticed one more awesome detail that set the two of us apart. "Uh... nice wings," I said.

Two webby black wings folded on either side of her spine, their tips brushing her lower calves. The wings protruded from two long slits that had been carelessly ripped in the layers of shirts.

Zach stared at the wings too. "What are you, a fairy?"

Charity laughed—a hard, raspy sound—and slapped her thighs. Zach and I exchanged looks. What the heck was so funny?

"Fairies are wispy and cute," J said. "Ethereal and filled with light—and, for the most part, well-behaved." He motioned toward Charity. "Clearly, *not* a fairy."

"Look who's dissing who. Any dragon worth his scales wouldn't live as a morph in a stupid box," Charity fired back. She spat out *morph* like it tasted bad. The two of them shot eye darts at each other for a moment before Charity turned her attention back to us. "I choose to call myself something altogether different. I..." she paused to add a theatric glare, "am a *fair-a-tude*."

Before I could think, my voice came out. "A *what*?"

"Fair-a-tude: a fairy with an attitude," Charity supplied. "A sprite with a snarl. A pixie with a past."

This trip to Camp Neece kept getting better and better. A slobbery dragon that ate sushi and a misfit whatever-she-was. Better than the beach with Olivia the Perfect. For sure.

CHAPTER SIX

The green dragon and fair-a-tude demolished the food in a few minutes. Not even a crumb left.

"If you don't live in the box, where do you live?" Zach asked.

Charity's thin shoulders lifted and fell. The foul aroma hit my nose again. Why did everything lately come with a nasty smell?

"Different places, different spaces. Where will Charity stay today? By the bay? In the hay?" Her words rang out like a song with a bizarre melody.

J gave Charity a disgusted look. "I don't like it when you respond in a riddle and a rhyme. Really, Charity. What harm would come from a straight answer?" J motioned to the Rainy Day Box. "She leaves something in lots of spots."

J's answer was as clear as mud too, and it rhymed besides. Charity huffed, then rummaged in the box and removed the pebble. As before when Zach had picked it up, the pebble turned into a large rock. She set it down and it puffed even larger. "I leave a touchstone."

"Touchstone?" Zach stared at the boulder as if he expected it to grow hairy arms and grab him.

"An object I can zero in on and figure my way back. A means to mark my place."

Zach considered. "Like an IP address."

Leave it to my brother to figure out the connection between a fair-a-tude's rock and computers. It did make sense though, sort of.

She twirled the end of a lock of hair with her fingers. "Or like breadcrumbs in one of those stupid old fairy tales. Most of the time, I hang out where my people are from... or used to be from." Charity's pale face shifted to a grey mask.

J's lips formed the word *no* at the exact moment Zach asked, "Where's that?"

When J circled his eyes, it reminded me of two green beach balls bobbing in the surf. "You just *had* to ask."

"Show ya!" Charity rested her hand on the touchstone and mumbled some words. The room went black. And we weren't in Aunt Neece's sunroom anymore.

I blinked and my eyes adjusted to catch any hint of light. The first thing I noticed was the same smell that clung to Charity like a nasty perfume, only a gazillion times worse. Zach glued himself to my side. He shivered. I willed myself to act all big sister and stay calm. Another boulder—I assumed one of Charity's touchstones—marked the spot at Charity's feet. Beyond that, I could see nothing but a lot of darkness.

Charity squatted and scratched around. Strange squeaky noises and mysterious skittering came from every direction. I heard a snap. Light flared. Charity held a thick stick, its end wrapped in flames. She slipped a box of matches into the torn pocket of her T-shirt.

"Let there be light," she said. I recognized that quote from the book of Genesis in the Bible. Did fair-a-tudes read?

J's upper lip curled. "Always stinks to the heavens here."

"Oh, and you don't?" Charity jabbed the torch in his direction.

"Careful with that, fairy. You'll burn something vital." J's brilliant eyes scanned the circle of pale yellow light. "While we're out here, I might as well go for a spin around the neighborhood. Been a few years since I worked my wings."

J's wings popped open like two halves of an umbrella. A slight breeze ruffled the skin stretched between the bony spines.

Zach still quivered beside me, but he loosened his grip on my waist a little.

J flapped three times. His wings caught and held the air, the way the sails billowed on the clipper ship we'd seen last summer when my family visited Boston harbor. The dragon lifted off and tucked his legs close to his body. The night sucked him in, a black vortex, and he faded from view. I missed J the moment my eyes could no longer detect his outline. But he was big enough to take care of himself. Zach and I needed to stick with Charity. Fair-a-tude or not, she was still a person, sort of, and this place was crazy freaky.

Charity sat down on a rock and picked slivers of bark from the torch handle. "Don't sweat it. That overgrown lizard will be back. He never strays far when he goes off on one of his so-called exercise flights." Charity's cheeks appeared even hollower in the torch light. Why the nasty attitude toward J? I noted the tips of her wings, then realized why they were black. They were scorched, and frayed so badly around the edges they looked brittle. Certainly, she wouldn't be able to fly. Sad.

"So, where are we?" I turned in place, my brother still plastered to my side, and strained to make out our surroundings. Strips of plastic, mounds of paper. It reminded me of Zach's room at home, where he stuffed dirty clothes behind the dresser and slung his baseball junk across the floor. The person in charge of this place hadn't picked up anything in a long, long time.

"The dump. The landfill. The glorious trash heap." Charity gestured with her free arm. "A giant gash in the earth filled with all the junk you—" she pointed an accusing finger toward us "—throw out."

Zach pushed away from me and stood with his hands on his hips. "*I* don't throw all *this* out."

Charity regarded my little brother with one corner of her lips crooked up. "During your life, little man, you will produce up to 4.6 pounds of refuse, trash, garbage per day. That's 140,700 pounds over your lifetime, about 70 tons. All your banana peels, your apple cores, your school papers, out-of-date computers, and phones." She took a breath and continued. "Ruined paper towels, out-grown clothes, shoes, and underwear. Your rusted cars, your wrecked boats, your pieces of houses, clippings from your yard, diapers from your babies, poop from your cats and dogs." She paused. "I don't have enough time to list it all."

"Gee. Guess I never thought about it. But, it has to go somewhere." My statement made sense.

Charity crossed her eyes at me. "Seventy tons, really?"

Aunt Neece recycled and kept fruit and vegetable peels, eggshells, and coffee grounds in a snap-lid jar, mulch for her garden. We did some of that back home, but my aunt barely threw away a toenail clipping.

"Won't do me much good to scream and scratch at you, I suppose." Charity fingered the C charm hanging from her necklace, like Aunt Neece did with her silver ring. "It won't bring my parents back. Won't help me find my sister."

A fair-a-tude sister? I hoped she wouldn't be as cranky as Charity.

A squeak split the darkness to our right. Charity spun around and held the torch aloft. Two glowing eyes peered from the garbage. Another squeak called from the opposite direction. Then another and another. Charity whipped the torch from one side to the next. Greedy, evil eyes watched us.

"Take this." She pushed the torch into my hand and grabbed a second stick with one end wrapped in dirty cloth. She touched the tip to the flames and the second torch whooshed to life.

We stood back to back, holding our lights. Charity's ruined wing tips twitched against my bare legs.

"Stand between us," I said to Zach, keeping my voice low.

He dug in his pocket, pulled out his knife, and flipped it open. Did he really think that two-inch blade stood a chance with whatever creature lurked behind those horrible eyes?

"Zach, I mean it—" Several more sets of eyes popped up around us. Their shadowy silhouettes suggested critters the size of the possums we had seen at the Junior Museum the last time we came to Camp Neece. My mind scrabbled to figure out what had us surrounded. Cats, dogs, rabbits?

"Rats," Charity said, as if I had asked the question aloud.

The first one, maybe the leader, inched forward until I could see its body. A long. bristled snout with a constantly twitching nose tested the air. A nappy body, twenty times the size of a pet store rat. And a skinny tail like an armadillo's, only black and filthy. And those eyes! It peered at us and let out a series of high-pitched squeaks. I didn't want to be anywhere near it, and especially not surrounded by a growing mob of its kin.

Zach let out a low growl. He switched his pocketknife to his left hand and pulled the Rainy Day Box toy sword from his pocket with his right hand. Oh yeah. That was going to scare them. Maybe it would work its magic here, too.

The tiny sword hummed, then swelled to its full war size. Torch light glinted from the blade. Zach's tendency to cram stuff in his pockets had finally come in handy. He stood there all brave, struggling to balance the sword, his little chest sticking out. Impressed me, but it didn't faze the rats. They inched closer, closer, closer.

A roar sounded from above, a screech like a locomotive's air brakes. I took my eyes off the rats long enough to glance into the darkness. Talons appeared first, then the full body of one clearly ticked-off dragon.

J hovered, his expansive wings whipping the torch fires into shifting arcs. He drew in a deep breath. The scales on his chest prickled and stood up. Then he opened his mouth. A stream of white-hot flames thundered from his lips and nose.

Rats scurried in every direction, except ours. In moments, only the scent of singed fur remained. I glanced down at my mood bracelet. It had turned dark red, total freak-out mode.

"Wow. Cool." Zach lowered his sword. "I totally get why dragons don't blow out their birthday candles."

J landed in one easy motion and folded his wings. "Please store those weapons, if you will. You know how I feel about violence."

Charity sneered. "Like the way you fried those rats? Very peaceful."

Thin wisps of smoke curled from his nostrils. "A harmless singeing to avoid a bloody altercation seemed prudent. I repeat, store those weapons."

Zach nodded. He pushed the single pocketknife blade back into its slot, then trained his gaze on the sword. It hummed and shrank down to its former size. How had my brother learned to control that? Back into his pockets, his treasures went. While he busied himself, Charity snuffed one torch and stepped away to stash it in an old metal footlocker at the edge of the trash heap.

J snapped off the point of one of his belly scales, then leaned down and whispered into my ear, "Take this. It will help keep you both safe when I can't." My eyes watered from his breath fumes, but I didn't pull away.

I turned the one-inch triangle of glassy green in my fingers. One of J's three thick upper eyelids slid down, then up. A dragon wink. Without speaking, I slipped the scale shard into my pocket. Charity rejoined us.

"Can we go home now?" J's eyes pleaded with Charity. "I'm a little winded—a bit out of shape, I'm afraid—and I could use some hors d'oeuvres."

Charity huffed, but extinguished and stored the other torch. She put her hands on the touchstone. I leaned in to hear her words. "Through stone. Through glass. Through time."

The dark wasteland of rubble around us rippled to gray, then Aunt Neece's sunroom shimmered. The skin on my arms and legs tingled, like the zing of static electricity. Zach stood beside me. Both of us blinked to adjust our eyes.

Two days earlier, we had passed the Leon County Landfill on our way to Aunt Neece's house. Was that the same odiferous place where Charity had taken us? No way to know for sure. But the nasty rodents—I'd never seen rats that big in real life.

Outside, the rain had stopped. Drops of water dangled from the leaves and glistened on the soggy grass. Everything looked cleansed and fresh, and steam rose from the tops of nearby houses.

"Where'd J and Charity go?" Zach asked.

I stepped over to the cedar chest and put my hand on the Rainy Day Box. Zach grabbed my arm. "Wait! You can't open it! It's not raining."

My hand rested on the jeweled box lid. I just wanted to do a quick check to make sure, but I had bent a Camp Neece rule when I smuggled the morph into the Capitol. Who knew how many bathrooms I'd have to clean for breaking *that* rule? I had to trust the fact that J had morphed back into his cramped home. But poor Charity. Was she alone in the dark somewhere, longing for her family? Where had the touchstone taken her?

The worry clung to me, then I shrugged it aside. That fair-a-tude wasn't just anybody. Charity was wherever and whenever she wanted to be. Would her "wherever and whenever" bring her back to the sunroom before Camp Neece ended for the summer? I hoped so. She was weird. But fascinating. Like I wanted to be.

CHAPTER SEVEN

My aunt cracked five eggs into a mixing bowl, added seasonings and milk, and gestured toward the bowl. Zach and I took turns using a whisk to whip the eggs into a "foamy froth" á la Food Channel. A pan of biscuits puffed in the oven, their tops turning a golden tan. Zach wanted confetti pancakes again, but I had begged for Aunt Neece's Special Eggs. Such an ordinary morning, after the landfill drama. My eyes burned. I had barely slept for dreaming about dragons and rats and a punk fairy who thought I had a cool watch.

Aunt Neece grabbed Zach and me in a smothering embrace. My entire family hugs. I was pretty used to it. But Aunt Neece clung on longer than usual, one of those hugs like she was afraid if she stopped, we'd disappear into nothing.

She finally let go, then grabbed a wet rag and wiped the kitchen counters like she was trying to rub holes in them. "Today, we're visiting Mission San Luis de Apalachee."

Zach raised one eyebrow and shot me a *what's-that* look. I didn't have a clue, but the Apalachee part sounded Native American, so Zach would be all over it. Me? I could stand a little mundane history after that landfill. Bet there were no mirrors there, no dark shadows to haunt my reflection. Another point for the win column.

Zach turned the bowl over to Aunt Neece. She poured the yellow mixture into a hot skillet, then added a half-dozen small chunks of cream cheese—the part that made her eggs so special.

"Here, Aidan. You can finish these up." She handed me the wooden spoon. The heat melted the cheese as I stirred. In a couple of minutes, the scrambled eggs steamed in the pan, perfect. I grabbed a potholder and moved the skillet so they wouldn't overcook, then turned off the burner.

Aunt Neece switched on the oven light, nodded, and asked Zach to hand her the insulated mitts. "Stand back!" She opened the door and a blast of hot bread-scented air whooshed out. Aunt Neece lifted the pan to the top of the stove and whumped the oven door shut with a hip.

"You kids have the table ready?"

"Yes ma'am!" we said together.

She used tongs to shift the biscuits onto our plates, added a generous heap of cooked eggs, and carried our filled plates to the round oak table, then went back for her own. "You want thumb-hole biscuits this morning?"

Zach and I bobbed our heads. Aunt Neece pressed her thumb into the middle of the biscuits, one by one, fast so she didn't feel the heat. We were big enough to punch our own thumb holes—we did that all the time at home—but something about having Aunt Neece do it made it special. Plus her thumb made larger craters for butter and honey.

Aunt Neece handed the bear-shaped honey dispenser to Zach. "I know you like to do this part."

Zach upended the honey bear and a ribbon of thick gold snaked out. He filled one biscuit, then the other before handing the honey bear to me. I dribbled tupelo honey in the impressions, then up and down the biscuits' sides in curly squiggles until Aunt Neece stopped me. Camp Neece Rule: no "playing" with the food. Though, pressing a thumb into a hot biscuit might qualify.

We dug into breakfast until the plates held only crumbs and a few curdles of eggs. I concentrated on my contented stomach and pushed aside any dark thoughts. No rats, no landfill, no fair-a-tude. Just breakfast as usual.

"Maybe that will hold you two until lunch." Aunt Neece stood and stored the honey and butter. She closed the refrigerator door and stood with her hands propped on her hips. "I can't believe all that sushi is gone. Again." She slid her squinted gaze from me to Zach. "One of you must have a hollow leg, is all I can figure."

I avoided looking at the guilty party, Zach the vacuum. Couldn't blame this one on J. That dragon didn't polish off two flats of California rolls. Not this time. What in the world would I feed J for hors d'oeuvres? Something fishy. Something that wouldn't send Aunt Neece back to the grocery store and "into the poorhouse." Mr. Pig bumped against my shins, angling for a handout. He had wolfed down his tuna feast, hogged down Sissy's leftovers, and trolled the floor for crumbs of our breakfast. I lifted a clump of scrambled egg from my plate and he licked it from my fingers.

"Can we use your computer, Aunt Neece?" I asked.

"After you do your kitchen chores, you *may*." She took the dirty skillet and the biscuit pan from the stovetop and filled them with soapy water. "Let these soak. I'll clean them later." She removed her cooking towel from her shoulder and draped it over the oven handle to dry. Any time my aunt entered the kitchen, she whipped a dish towel over one shoulder. Mama cooked the same way. Runs in the family.

As soon as we loaded the dishwasher and wiped the table, Zach and I trailed after her to a small office where she operated her home business. At Camp Neece, computer time came seldom, and with—wait for it—rules. Zach didn't understand why we had a separate "visitor" password, or why my aunt and our parents had installed Parental Controls, but I did. The Internet brimmed with knowledge and pictures and cool stuff. But it was scary too, like Charity's landfill. Evil rats lurked around every corner, and no fire-breathing green dragon would swoop in to protect us.

"There you go. Just don't mess with any of my work papers." Aunt Neece checked the time on the chicken-shaped wall clock. "Thirty minutes. I'll take my shower. When I get through, you two need to get ready." She left the room.

I typed *dragon* into the search bar like I'd done many times before and a gazillion listings popped up. One site showed pictures of the different types of dragons, where they had lived, and their long history dating back to 4000 B.C. Many I had seen, so I scrolled past them. I spotted one newer website that linked dragon colors to their characteristics.

"Who knew they came in so many different shades?" I said. I clicked on Green Dragon. Zach and I scanned the page.

"This doesn't sound anything like J." Zach frowned. "Says green dragons are liars, and what's be-leg-er... rent?"

"Belligerent. Means you're angry and like to argue." I read more. About how green dragons lived in the deep woods near water, liked to eat elf flesh, and breathed poisonous chlorine gas. "Like Aunt Neece says, you can't believe everything you read on the Internet." I wasn't buying any of that belligerent stuff. My mood bracelet slid down my wrist and clacked against the computer mouse. I checked its color: light blue, peaceful and relaxed.

"J doesn't look anything like any of these dragons," Zach said. "Dragons are supposed to be bigger than this whole house." He drew a wide circle with his arms. "And all fire-breathing and like, bite people in half."

And J ate sushi and Swiss cake rolls. "Well, maybe things have changed since back then. Besides, how do we know for sure all those legends are for real?"

"Yeah," Zach said, "and until a couple of days ago, we didn't know dragons were real either."

But I'd known. Somehow, I'd always known.

Zach jumped up and struck a karate pose. "I'd do battle with a dragon. I'd stab it with my sword and save the day!" He jabbed the air with his imaginary weapon, then stuck his chest out and propped his hands on his hips, all Mr. Superhero.

"Oh sure you would."

"Or..." He swung around and held his arms in front of him, fists clenched tight. "I'd bonk it and make it fall out. One whack, right here." He poked a spot between his own eyes.

"You will not whack *anything*." I wiggled a finger at him. "Sit. You're wasting our computer time."

Zach plopped down with a huff, then we searched other websites filled with dragon lore. Much of the stuff, I'd seen, but Zach hadn't, and he insisted on looking.

Depending on where they lived—either in the East, in China, or in the West, in Europe—dragons were seen as either good or evil. J had to be a Chinese dragon—known for protecting and bringing wealth and good fortune. The ones in Europe were fierce and warriors hunted them down.

One website told of a Native American legend, of a snake-like being with wings. Maybe the Native Americans at the mission had such a legend. Dragons, or the myth of dragons, stretched around the world, to every continent except Antarctica. I didn't blame them on that one. Who wanted to live where it was so cold all the time, especially when a dragon had an internal fire to stoke. But how much of this stuff was true? Who's to say someone hadn't made most of it up, for fun?

J was for real. My aunt's mangled sunroom proved it. Our imaginations wouldn't dissolve wall paint and leave a scorch mark on the rug. And why hadn't Aunt Neece said anything about that? She noticed everything. Either my aunt was slipping, or I wasn't the only one keeping secrets.

I reached my hand into my shorts pocket and touched the triangular piece of J's scale. Real.

Aunt Neece pulled into the parking lot at Mission San Luis in front of a modern brick building. Dullsville. I glanced at my mood bracelet, expecting it to be pale white, the color for bored, and it was. Though I had warmed to the notion of *not* being excited earlier, I doubted my wish now. All this educational business had worked my last nerve. I'd rather be back in my aunt's back yard, making sure my tan wouldn't fade before school started. Hot air slammed me in the face as soon as I stepped from the car. I could be home sitting in a cool room, recording amazing wisdom into my journal. Better, I could be spending time with J, or Charity.

I huffed out a breath, got out of the car, and tagged behind my aunt and brother.

"I've ridden by this place every day for years and always wanted to stop." Aunt Neece held open the glass entrance door and a blast of chilled air greeted us. At least if I had to tromp around a museum, it was air-conditioned. I spotted a gift shop with T-shirts, books, and jewelry. My day brightened.

Aunt Neece must've noted the gleam in my eyes. She turned me away from the brightly lit shop. "Let's see everything else before you spend your fun-money."

I resigned myself to rooms and rooms, and endless displays of old junk. When we stepped inside the main part of the museum, an area no bigger than Aunt Neece's lower floor awaited us. Aunt Neece had shelled out bucks for this? That money could've bought enough sushi to take care of J for at least a couple of days. Or she could've just handed it over for the gift shop, and we could have gone back to the house.

The museum part took twenty minutes. I liked the pottery and fossils, and Zach fixated on the tools. The Apalachee Indians had lived here, along with the Spanish missionaries way back in 1656. No evidence of any dragon legends here, either on the walls or stashed in the pullout exhibit drawers. I studied the map of the grounds. Oh dread, this building was only a small part of the mission's museum. Most of it lay outside, beyond a set of glass doors. And with Aunt Neece in charge, we would definitely be going through those doors. Maybe the other buildings held some mention of dragons.

A sticky wall of heat attacked my face when I stepped into the open air. An angry purple smudge highlighted the sky in the west.

"We best skip to what we really want to see," my aunt said. "That storm will be here in an hour or so."

Rain! Zach glanced over to me, wide-eyed. I read the dragon-thoughts in his expression. I felt my lips curl into a smile.

Zach dashed in front of us to the first structure, the council house. We ducked through a low entrance. The crude building reminded me of an overgrown circus tent, only made with rough logs and palmetto fronds, with dirt for a floor. Massive tree trunks formed the support beams. I doubted Zach or I could reach around them, even if we joined hands.

"Wow," Zach and I said at the same time.

"It's 120 feet in diameter and can hold up to 3000 people," Aunt Neece read from the brochure.

My eyes scanned the immense circle, imagining all those Native Americans crammed in the space. A girl about my age in long dark braids, buckskins, and beads stepped up, one of the many museum guides dressed in period costume. Or I thought she was at first, until she got closer and I saw her face. Charity!

She acted like she didn't know me or Zach, and it was totally okay for her to be a guide at some dumb museum. How did she hide her wings? When she turned sideways, I saw the cape. Clever, Charity. Zach took one quick look at her, didn't react at all, then dashed ahead of us.

As we strolled around an outside ring bordered by elevated platforms on our right and long tables on our left, Charity-in-disguise told us about daily life in the settlement, pointed out where the Apalachee people prepared hides, cooked, and slept.

"My people kept a roaring fire lit here." She stood in front of a tall pile of logs in the center of the council house. I craned my neck to see the center of the roof directly overhead. A large hole opened to the sky, a place to allow the smoke, or a dragon, to escape.

"Didn't it rain in?" Zach asked the same question I thought.

"No. The heat from the fire was enough to evaporate any water before it could hit the ground below." Charity's lips twitched when she saw the wonder on Zach's upturned face.

Guess she was getting a huge kick out of the whole guide ruse.

I played along, looked up at the roof vent again. If we cut a hole in Aunt Neece's sunroom, J could breathe fire and keep the rain from hitting the rug, I'd just bet. Too bad those Apalachee folks didn't have their own dragon. It would've saved a lot of work gathering firewood.

Zach dashed from one hide preparation table to the next. "Look. This hide is from a white-tailed deer! Oh, and a coyote pelt!" He yammered on and on. "A cowhide. How cool."

A slight movement caught my attention and I moved away from the preparation tables. A little snake eyed me from its spot between two dried palmetto fronds in the thatched wall. I stepped closer to get a better look and went through the critter-danger checklist my woodsman daddy had taught me. Rounded pupils, and tan and dark olive blotchy patches—a young gray rat snake. No need to screech alarm. No doubt it feasted on the small rodents living in and around the council house.

Another reptile joined the snake—a garden anole, displaying its brown color to match the surroundings. Two more lizards popped their heads from cracks. The snake and lizards eyed me as if I was the tourist attraction. I checked the wall nearby to see more round eyes peering in my direction.

So, was I going to start seeing snakes and lizards everywhere, like I did with dragons?

"Aidan," Aunt Neece called. "Keep up, hon."

"Yes," Charity said. "You wouldn't want to *miss* anything."

I turned my head toward them, then gave the reptile audience one more glance. One by one, the lizards slipped back into their hidey-holes. The snake stayed put.

"Don't worry. I'm not going to tell anyone you're here," I said in a low voice. People could be cruel to snakes, killing them without thought. Fear drove the reaction. They'd do the same with dragons, too. But not if I could stop it.

I jogged a few steps to catch up with my aunt and brother.

Our fair-a-tude guide followed us around the circle and told of huge powwows before the natives' ball games. She held out a pottery bowl of yaupon holly leaves. "They roasted and ground them, then brewed *cassina*, a black drink loaded with caffeine. The drink could only be served in the council house unless the chief gave his permission." Had to give it to Charity. She knew her history.

"Good thing Zach can't have any," I said to Aunt Neece. "He's hyper enough."

The ghosts of those Apalachee people swirled around me, drinking cassina, whooping it up, eating fish, game, squash and corn, and sleeping. It sounded a lot like a tailgate party for a Florida State football game. Our family didn't get that rowdy before the games, only stood around eating chicken from a bucket, but others around us did.

"As females, you and I wouldn't be allowed into the natives' form of ballgame," Charity said. "Only the male warriors did that. They'd play with fifty or more, and the game sometimes grew violent and resulted in... death." Charity's lips slid into a strange smile.

A shiver noodled my spine. Charity could be a fierce friend, or a horrid enemy, my inner advisor warned.

Too bad the Apalachee couldn't have added in an immense green dragon, like J. Swooping down in the middle of the game, firing blasts of flame across the players. Game over. Hope they had a supply of fish to pay the dragon for his help. But then, J hated violence, so forget that.

Aunt Neece took our picture with the "guide," then we thanked her and stepped outside. I turned around to give Charity a little secret wave. She was gone.

"There's one of the goals." Aunt Neece pointed to a tall post with a woven triangle at the top. "I'd hate to have to hit that." She read the brochure. "The game ball was made from hardened clay covered with buckskin, and only about the size of a golf ball."

Zach picked up a hickory nut and reared back. Aunt Neece stopped him before he could hurl it toward the goal.

Thunder rumbled in the distance. The air hung heavy, thick with the promise of an impending downpour. We took a quick tour of the fort, though Zach could've spent all day talking to the dude who looked like a movie pirate. Then we stopped by the blacksmith hut and watched another man fire and pound a metal wall hook. His helper pumped two large bellows to blow air across the coals. I half expected Charity to show up again, but she didn't.

Aunt Neece motioned for us to pose by the church doorway. I swatted Zach's hand when he tried to hold devil-fingers over my head.

When we entered the large sanctuary—a white building made from hand-cut logs and stucco—I noticed a high-pitched squeaking. Spirits of the Spanish missionaries? Aunt Neece peered into the dark rafters overhead. "Sounds like bats."

The skin on my neck prickled. Aunt Neece walked farther into the church, studying the painted icons and checking the pamphlet for information. Zach and I circled, our faces upturned to the dark ceiling.

A shadow shifted—larger than any bat I'd ever seen on the Animal Channel. Black wings unfurled. A scaly head tipped to stare down to where we stood, its glaring silver eyes penetrating the gloom. My spit dried in my mouth and I couldn't speak. I ripped my gaze from the figure and looked toward Zach. He grinned, his eyes scanning the rafters. Didn't he see that huge dark dragon? I jerked my head back toward the ceiling. It was still there.

The creature dropped down, its legs fully extended. I gasped and managed a small squeak. Ebony scales glinted in the sprinkles of dim light that pierced cracks in the walls. A gust of hot, foul air stung my nose. Talons! Sharp!

Without really thinking, I slipped my hand into my pocket, found J's scale shard, and lifted it out. The green triangle vibrated in my palm.

"There's one," Zach said in a loud whisper. "See it? It's hiding behind that one board."

I blinked a few times and searched for the dark figure. Gone. Eyes played tricks sometimes. All this dragon business was getting to me. Shake it off, Aidan.

Aunt Neece appeared beside us. "Sounds like this place is one big bat house."

Weren't bats like flying rats? I pictured Charity and those mutant landfill rats and shivered. I returned J's scale to my pocket.

"Bats are beneficial," she said, never missing a chance for a teachable moment. "One bat can eat up to a thousand bugs and mosquitoes every night."

Zach pranced around beside me like he had to pee. "Do you think a dragon might come in here to sleep at night?" he asked.

Aunt Neece squinted into the dim light, then down at Zach. "Why in the world would you ask that?"

Zach lifted his shoulders and let them drop. "Uh... no reason." He spun around and dashed out the door. A few raindrops pelted the already-wet dirt at the church entrance. Aunt Neece lifted one eyebrow and turned to me for an explanation. I held up my palms like *I don't have a clue.*

"I *told* Mama he was watching way too much Sci-Fi," I said.

"Well, your brother best watch that imagination of his. It could land him in a heap of trouble."

CHAPTER EIGHT

As soon as we jumped into the car and strapped on our seat belts, the rain poured. The wipers whipped full-blast and barely cleared the sheeting water.

"Guess we shouldn't have taken time to hit the gift shop." I shot my aunt my most sincere *I'm-sorry* look. In truth, I wasn't a bit sorry about the rain.

I had begged to ride shotgun—big as I was now, she couldn't claim the air bags might smash me into oblivion in an accident. We wasted twenty whole minutes sitting in the car with the wipers beating until the rain slacked off and Aunt Neece decided to make a break for home.

Zach sat in the back seat, jabbering on and on about deer skinning and bats and the ironsmith's bellows. Maybe he was trying to take our minds off the horrible storm, or his dumb comment about dragons. Maybe he was trying to drive me and Aunt Neece nutso—in which case, he was doing a good job.

My mood bracelet showed orange with a rim of red: a little worried and stressed. A truck plowed by in the next lane, sending a waterfall arching across the windshield. The wipers struggled to regain control.

At the intersection, my aunt slowed, though the light was green. She looked both ways before accelerating. The black van came from nowhere. I'd always doubted people's stories about things "appearing from thin air," but that's exactly what happened. I turned my head to the right. The van bore down on us, its grill grinning like some hungry, angry beast. A rooster tail of water shot out from its flanks. Sugar!

My hand reached instinctively for the shard of J's scale in my pocket. The van jerked to a crawl, as if it had hit a force field. So many times in movies, I had watched fight scenes where the bullets whizzed in for the kill then hung in mid-air, allowing the hero to step out of the way in the nick of time. They could do those special effects in movies and on TV. Only this was no movie.

I opened my mouth to call out. My lips wouldn't work and my tongue had frozen in place. My ears hummed. My skin tingled. The air around the car shimmered.

Then we were on the opposite side of the intersection. I snapped to attention, like I had awakened from a nightmare. Zach sang some little ditty in the back seat, palming the chert rock arrowhead he had purchased in the gift shop. Aunt Neece's hands gripped the steering wheel and her eyes focused on the road. But she wasn't as freaked out as she should've been, not after almost getting smashed to bits.

I spun around to see where the black van had gone and caught only its glowing red tail lights, growing distant in the drumming rain.

On my wrist, the mood bracelet showed a calm blue green. Must be broken.

We reached Aunt Neece's subdivision, our turn, the driveway, the dry garage. The engine ticked and water vapor rose from the hood after she turned the key.

"Home to Camp Neece, safe and sound," my aunt announced.

Zach made zooming noises. "Bet it would be fun to ride a motorcycle in all that rain."

My aunt's eyes flicked to the rearview mirror. She unbuckled her safety belt. "I'll do everything in my power to convince you not to ever ride one of those machines, young man. Too dangerous!"

Dangerous? And almost getting T-boned by a stop-light-running van wasn't? My mouth hung open and I snapped it shut before either of them noticed. I hadn't imagined that black van, but they obviously hadn't seen anything.

Zach pulled an eye roll. "What's for dinner?"

"That stew I put in the slow cooker this morning before you two goons climbed out of bed, that's what." Aunt Neece herded us into the house. I carried a bag with my one purchase—a pale blue Mission San Luis T-shirt.

Inside, I could still hear the steady thrum of rain on the sunroom roof. Good! I hoped, hoped, hoped it would hold out until I could see J and Charity. Maybe she'd answer some questions, like why, and how, she had appeared at the museum.

"Mind if I take a quick nap?" Aunt Neece asked. "The heat wears me out."

I looked at Zach and tried to act casual. "Sure."

She headed for the living room, to her favorite worn recliner. "I'm right here if you need me."

"Like, if we cut off a limb?" Zach asked.

"Yes, like that," Aunt Neece turned around and said with a tired smile. "Make yourselves a snack to hold you until dinner." Zach and I loomed at the threshold between the two rooms until she settled into her chair. In a few moments, I heard the gentle low rumble of her snores.

"What'll we do?" Zach asked. "We ate the rest of the sushi last night."

"Correction: *you* ate the rest of the sushi." I tipped my head in the direction of the cupboard. "I have an idea."

J's pleased rumble sounded deep in his throat, a noise like the idle of Daddy's 4-wheeler engine. "The hors d'oeuvres are marvelous today."

My eyes dared Zach to rat me out. Hey, tuna cat food nachos counted as fish. "Glad you like them. They're a bit different than the ones I usually make."

"You have the makings of a gourmet, my dear. Perhaps you watch the Food Channel." J dribbled a dollop of cat food down his belly scales. "Oopsie." It landed on the rug and Mr. Pig gobbled it down.

Too bad I couldn't sew. I'd make a dragon-sized bib. Zach put one of J's special nachos on the rug. Mr. Pig hunkered down to enjoy the delicacy. Guess no harm would come from a treat made with a corn chip, cat food tuna, and a sprinkle of melted cheese. Mr. Pig smacked and purred at the same time.

Sissy strolled into the sunroom. She regarded J with round yellow eyes. She rarely meowed, unlike Mr. Pig who fussed and commented about everything.

J lowered his huge head to Sissy's level. I gasped. Sissy stood, stretched and nose-bumped the dragon. "Glad you could join us, little shy one," J said.

"You act like you know the cats," I said. My heart settled into a slower pace.

J lifted his head back to my level. "Why wouldn't I? We share the same abode." His eyes shifted to the jeweled box. "I prefer the felines to that nasty little dark fairy who drops in uninvited. Charity is a troublesome being best avoided if you—"

My brother dug one hand into the Rainy Day Box. He picked up something small. J's emerald eyes widened. "I wouldn't take that out if—"

Too late. Zach held up a cat's eye marble to what little light filtered through the rain-soggy sky. "Wonder what this does."

J jerked back to his full height. "You had to ask." He snorted and tiny puffs of stinky steam curled from his nostrils.

The air in the room rippled. The sunroom floor shifted slightly side to side, as if a minor earthquake shook the house. The marble lifted from Zach's palm and started to spin, slowly at first, then building speed until I could no longer make out the topaz cat's eye coloration in the middle.

Charity popped into the room. One minute, she wasn't there. The next, she stood in front of us with her hands akimbo on her skinny hips. Her clothes were, if possible, more stained than before and the nauseating scent of the landfill hung around her, a moldy invisible cloak. Maybe she should've kept the Native American costume.

Her face, blackened like war paint, trailed with long streaks where tears had washed the skin beneath her eyes almost clean.

"You okay?" I asked.

Zach stared at the now-calm marble in his palm. "Hey—that was cool."

J snuffled. "Why you feel creating a disturbance is a good thing is beyond me, Charity. Why not a hurricane, or at least a very rousing tropical storm?"

"One must make a grand entrance." Charity dragged her sleeve across her runny nose. "Or, an unexpected one."

I strained to hear any noise from the living room. Aunt Neece's rhythmic snores called from inside the house. I took a deep breath to calm my nerves.

"Guess the marble is yours. Another touchstone?" I asked.

Charity held out her palm to Zach and he handed over the cat's eye. "Hardly. It's not even a stone—touch*stone*, get it?" She trained her eyes on the marble. This time, instead of spinning, it grew until it reached the size of a cantaloupe. "It's my seer's mirror."

A misty whorl of silvery blue filled the orb, reminding me of the glass gazing ball in Aunt Neece's garden.

"Is it magic?" Zach whispered, watching the smoky breath swirl inside the orb.

"Isn't everything?" Charity pulled a clown face; her eyes crossed, her tongue stuck out and waggling. On her, the visage looked out of place.

Something new moved inside of the sphere. Charity stopped goofing off and leaned in. Zach bunched up beside me and we stared at the orb. I felt the presence—smelled it too—of J close over my shoulder, watching.

Seeing the scene unfolding within the overgrown marble was like viewing a miniature 3-D movie. The figure—a young girl with wispy silver wings and hair the color of butterscotch—sat on the dirt with her legs drawn to her chest, and her face buried in her hands.

"Who's that?" Zach reached out to touch the ball, but his finger tapped against an invisible field. He jabbed three more times. The air resisted his attempts.

"Be careful, Mr. Touch Everything! I set up a protection zone," Charity snapped. "Otherwise, you'd get a nasty shock."

Zach drew back his hand and crammed it into his pocket. One day, if he lived long enough, my brother might "learn to curb his impulses," as Mama put it.

J idly strummed Mr. Pig's coat with one talon. The rotund tabby looked up at the dragon with sleepy, pleased eyes. Sissy butted J's leg and he reached his other front foot down to noodle her head. Guess Zach and I were the only ones excited about a marble turning into a seer's mirror.

"That," Charity said, pointing to the tiny female figure inside the globe, "is my sister Faith. And I must find her soon." Her voice sounded strained, as if she might cry any moment. "Or it will be too late."

"Late, schmate," J mumbled.

I gave him a look over my shoulder. Charity wasn't kidding. Anyone could see her sister was in trouble.

CHAPTER NINE

For the next hour, the rain continued. Charity tapped the seer's mirror to scroll from one horrible scene to the next, following her sister through dark tunnels and rooms with shadows. We looked for clues, anything to help Charity figure out where her sister had wandered.

I heard the slap-slam of Aunt Neece's recliner. "Aidan? Zach!"

"Coming!" I yelled. Zach and Mr. Pig jumped up and lumbered in the direction of the kitchen. Sissy shot off into the house, fast for such an old cat. I searched the sunroom for any lingering evidence of a dragon or fair-a-tude.

J and Charity had vanished. Again. All of this coming and going, and appearing and disappearing, made me tired and edgy.

"You kids hungry?" Aunt Neece stretched and yawned at the door to the sunroom. She stepped aside for Zach and Mr. Pig. "What am I saying, of course you're hungry." She spun around and headed into the kitchen. "Wash your hands and come help me get dinner on the table."

The churning feeling in my stomach wasn't due to hunger, but worry about Charity's sister. What would happen if Charity couldn't find her? I had to help. Maybe the rain would continue a little longer, and Aunt Neece would take another nap. Anything! I glanced at the Rainy Day Box and let out a long sigh. Then I shrugged and walked into the kitchen.

I chopped veggies for the salad while Aunt Neece cut thick slices of multigrain bread for toast. What a team we made. If only I could ask her what to do about Charity. She'd always helped me with my problems before, even things I didn't share with my parents.

Zach set the table. Napkin on the left with the fork. Knife and spoon on the right. Space in the middle for the plate. Three summers ago at Camp Neece, proper place settings and table etiquette had been frequent teachable moments. Zach slipped from time to time and propped his elbows on the table, or dropped food on his clothes, but he managed to chew with his mouth closed and keep his napkin across his lap most of the time.

Bet J would upset Aunt Neece with his drooling. The table would dissolve. I smiled, thinking about the big green lug hunkered over his plate with a string of napkins lashed around his neck.

"Aunt Neece, may I ask you a question?" I removed the wilted lettuce leaves and cucumber peels from the cutting board and dumped them into the glass jar bound for the mulch bin.

"Absolutely. If I don't have a good answer, I'll make one up." She laughed at her own joke.

"If a friend's in trouble and you know you might be able to help, should you?" I tossed the greens with the other veggies and shook croutons on top. "Even if it might be a little... dangerous?"

She regarded me with one of those stares that made me feel like she could read my mind.

"Is this hypothetical?"

"I don't know what that means."

"Hypothetical means—" she gestured with a wooden spoon "—not real. Setting up a situation in your mind to figure out how you might resolve it."

"Oh." I got it. Kind of like writing fantasy.

"It *is* hypothetical, isn't it? Or do I need to worry?" She watched for my reaction.

I shook my head. "All good."

She lifted the toasted bread from the oven and forked it onto our plates, then added generous portions of the stew. My mouth watered. Nothing beat Aunt Neece's stew with its velvety brown gravy, tender chunks of meat, and those yummy potatoes and carrots. My stomach rolled a bit, part hunger, part still a nervous mess from the last dragon and fair-a-tude visit.

Zach and I carried the loaded plates, salads, and iced tea to the table.

"Helping out is what friends are for," my aunt said, "as long as it doesn't bring harm to you, your brother, or your family." She paused before she added, "There are some people who exist to create drama, wreak havoc, and stir up life until you can't tell which end is up. Be watchful of that kind of person." My aunt stared at me long and hard. "She, or he, is *not* a friend."

Charity was full of drama, sure, but it was because of her life. Not like she created it. Charity needed me.

We bowed our heads and Zach said the blessing—so fast, his words jammed together and I wondered if the prayer even made it past the ceiling. I speared a chunk of venison and popped it into my mouth. The blended flavors of venison and seasonings wrapped around my tongue. The queasy feeling from before calmed a little. How I wished I could let

Charity sit with us at this table, eating stew and salad, and sopping up gravy with thick toast. Maybe she wouldn't look so starved, or so sad.

As soon as we ate and cleared the dishes, I leaned over to look from the kitchen window. The rain had stopped. Steam rose from the ground. There'd be no helping a "hypothetical" friend today.

Mama called promptly at seven. Aunt Neece shared the two goofy pictures from the day and they talked a bit before Zach and I took turns.

"Have you decided what kind of party you want for your thirteenth birthday?" Mama asked. "It's only two short months off. We'll need to send invitations early to reserve the date."

Why turning thirteen was such a colossal deal defied me. Now, fifteen? Fifteen would be huge! I could get my restricted driver's permit. Sixteen? Even better, when I got my full license. Eighteen would bring high school graduation and, *gasp*, college. Thirteen seemed dull as dirt by comparison.

"We don't have to do anything big," I said.

My mama paused on the other end. I could imagine her picking up a strand of her blonde hair and twirling it around one finger, the way she does when she's mulling over something. "Honey, thirteen *is* a big deal in *our* family."

By nine o'clock, Zach had worn Aunt Neece to a frazzle. He lunged from the sofa to the floor, to the sofa, to the recliner and back. Sissy hissed and dashed down the hall to hide beneath a bed. Mr. Pig vaulted onto the top level of the kitty playhouse and watched from inside one carpeted cubicle.

"You snuck one of your soft drinks, didn't you?" Aunt Neece asked.

Zach grinned and showed his teeth like a hyena. Yep, a sure sign he had hit the sugar lode.

She blew out a breath and looked at me. "Did you and your bouncy brother write a thank-you card to Miz Bridie?"

"No ma'am."

"Good time to do that." Aunt Neece walked to the back of the house and returned with a stack of cards and envelopes. "Pick one you like. I'll make sure to give it to her at our next writers' group meeting."

I fanned out the cards on the kitchen table. Zach buzzed around me like an annoying fly, snatching first one card then the next. Sugar and little brothers don't mix. Note to self: be sure to remind Aunt Neece to hide the little cooler with the canned drinks.

I chose a card with a watercolor of a wolf. Bright, bold colors. Miz Bridie would like it. After I wrote a short note and signed my name, I drew little hearts and flowers on the envelope. Not to be outdone, Zach grabbed the crayons and busied himself with an elaborate drawing of a flying dragon. Not bad for a computer whiz kid.

"Don't forget to sign your name, kiddo," I said.

"I'm not a kiddo. I'll be eleven in eight months."

"Big whoop."

Zach shoved the card into its decorated envelope and dashed into the living room to deliver it to Aunt Neece. I trailed behind him. Of course she exclaimed over our artwork like we were famous. She stared at Zach's dragon with a sad, weird expression, like she was seeing something from far, far away.

"Shower, tooth brushing, then to bed." She took one last look at Zach's drawing and pointed to the back of the house. "Tonight, Zach, you go first."

My brother shot from the room. I smiled at my aunt. Quiet had never sounded so good.

I wandered into the sunroom. The sun had finally set and only a scrim of orange painted the western horizon. The garden lights popped on, illuminating the birdbath, the flower gardens, and the slate pathways that wound between them. In one corner, my aunt had planted a "moon garden." All of the flowers were white or pale yellow. During the few nights when the moon was full, their petals seemed to glow with reflected light. I had seen it once, last year during Camp Neece. But the moon wouldn't be full for three more weeks. Too bad.

The Rainy Day Box sat on its perch, just an old beat-up wooden box. I stepped toward the cedar chest, then stopped. Nothing might happen if I opened it, but something might. I'd skated past the rules before. Maybe I'd harm J or Charity. Maybe I, Aunt Neece, or Zach would get hurt. Too many maybes. I brushed my hand over the lid as I walked by and it felt cold.

Instead of opening the box, I folded myself into one of the cushioned rockers. The gentle back and forth motion usually calmed me, but not this time. Thoughts flitted through my brain, bumping into each other. I worried about Charity. How did she find food? Did she pick out her meals from the garbage, like she did her clothing? And what about her sister? She was lost in some hideous place and I only had one more day left here.

If I didn't help Charity, who would?

CHAPTER TEN

"What's on the Camp Neece agenda for today?" I whipped eggs and milk together in a shallow bowl, this time for French toast.

Aunt Neece cut several thick slices of sourdough bread with a long serrated knife while the skillet heated. "Since this is our last day together, I thought we'd do something very old-Florida."

My mind raced. What did she mean by *old* Florida? Would we wrestle alligators? Ride through some deep swamp on an airboat? No theme parks—Aunt Neece called them "canned fun." Had to be a way I could duck out, stay home, and help Charity. Somehow, I'd find a time.

Zach forked a slice of bread and slapped it into the egg mixture. Slime splattered everything.

"You could do that a little less enthusiastically, son." Aunt Neece used a paper towel to mop up the spilled yolks. "Flip it over and coat the other side. Slowly this time."

He lifted one corner of his lip, but for once didn't say something smarty. Aunt Neece helped guide his hand so he wouldn't slop egg juice when he moved the bread to the skillet.

"I can do this, Aunt Neece," I said.

"I know you can, Aidan. You're turning into quite the little cook. But your brother has to learn too." She thought a moment. "Okay, maybe you can share toast duty."

Zach and I dipped the bread, then I transferred the pieces to the pan, turned them to brown both sides, and moved them to a warm plate at the rear of the stove. Aunt Neece cooked turkey bacon and sliced fresh pineapple. When we had a tall stack of cooked toast, she loaded three plates and set them on the table.

"Today, we're going to Wakulla Springs." Aunt Neece took a slurp of coffee.

"Isn't that where they have those glass-bottomed boats?" I poured thick cane syrup over my buttered French toast, then handed the bottle to Zach. He drowned his plate, even the fruit and bacon.

"They do, but they're not operating right now. All the rain has made the water a little dark, with runoff from the nearby swamps and streams." She cut a wedge of toast and popped it into her mouth. "I think they still have the jungle cruises."

Zach wallowed his toast in the syrup. Good thing we'd be busy today. My brother would be on a wall-banging sugar high for hours.

"There's plenty to see, all the same. We'll take the masks and snorkels." She took a noisy sip of coffee. Every day, she had at least two cups—her *Go-Juice*. "Hope the rain holds off. Maybe we'll get in a few hours before it runs us home."

I thought of J, cramped in that box. And Charity. No way I'd back out of some quality sun time. I felt a little guilty for being excited about spending the day at a spring, when Charity was in her world, dirty, hungry, and searching for her missing sister. I'd find time for her. One way or the other.

There was always tonight.

When we arrived at the state park, only a handful of people shared the sandy beach next to the springs. Aunt Neece made a beeline to a level spot beneath a stand of cypress trees. We unloaded three chairs, a rolling cooler, and two carryalls filled with towels, sunscreen, and bags of chips. Zach took one look at the dive tower and raced off as soon as Aunt Neece had slathered him with sunscreen.

"No diving!" my aunt called after him. She plopped down and grabbed a novel from her bag. "I know there are lifeguards on duty. Still, help me keep an eye on that boy."

"Yes, ma'am."

With the sketchpad opened in my lap, I held a charcoal pencil and took in the beauty of Wakulla Springs. Across the water on the spring's far shore, a great blue heron blended into the tall marsh grass. The richness and variety of colors amazed me. The tree line was dappled with hues of green. High, wispy clouds moved lazily overhead. For once, dark storm clouds didn't mar the sky. I couldn't open the box to help Charity, even if I was at the house.

This place didn't seem the sort of hangout for an evil dragon, but neither had the grocery store or the governor's office or the museum. I took a deep breath and let it out slowly through pursed lips, then reached inside my carryall to touch the zippered pouch containing J's shard. Two more breaths in and out, and the peace of the springs tamped down my worries.

The water was the shade of weak tea, but the white sandy bottom still showed within the shallow part of the swimming area. Beyond the floating ropes and buoys, the water turned avocado green from the ribbons of grass undulating below the surface in the gentle current. A toddler laughed nearby, digging holes in the wet sand with a yellow plastic shovel.

A slight breeze pushed chilled air across my skin and sent miniature ripples across the mirrored surface of the water. When I allowed my eyes to go slightly unfocused, I picked out the quick darting movements of dragonflies flitting between the above-ground cypress roots—the cypress *knees*—surrounding our little day camp, and overhead in the fresh-scented air. A green darner landed on the arm of my folding chair and watched me with its bulbous multiple-lens eyes. Was this *ode* a dragon in disguise?

This place, full of light and sound and good scents, was so different from where Charity had to live. How could I sit *here*, loving every second, when she had to stay *there*? But then, she had appeared at the museum. Why not stay with me?

My ears caught the caw of a crow, an occasional cricket song, the calls of coots and wood ducks skimming among the lily pads, and a mullet slapping the surface after jumping skyward. An anhinga skimmed low over the spring and river, landed with a splash, then dove under the water. It reappeared with a small fish clamped in its beak. The bird flipped back its head, swallowed the catch whole, and let out a cackle.

I sketched furiously to stop the other gloomy thoughts. I outlined the trees with their hanks of moss for the background, then added a twig with a dragonfly perched on the tip in the front. I took care to use faint lines for the webbing on its wings.

Then that shadowy place from the seer's mirror invaded my thoughts again. The peaceful image evaporated and other, darker scenes shoved into my mind's eye. Black talons ripping the air, searching for... what? Chunks of green, brown, and black raining down, a frenzy of blood and fury. My hand followed my imagination's lead, until the pencil's tip nearly cut into the paper.

"What are you drawing over there?" Aunt Neece asked.

"Um... nothing." I tore out the page, folded it in half, and crammed it in the back of the pad. I flicked a smile her way. "I get a little intense sometimes."

I took a deep breath and worked on pastel thoughts. Nothing dark. Nothing scary. Between strokes of my pencil, I glanced up and caught Zach bounding up the cement stairs and plummeting into the deep springs that fed the Wakulla River. First he jumped feet-first from the lower level, technically *not* a dive. After climbing out of the water, he skittered to the top platform and waited his turn until the lifeguard signaled that the last swimmer had cleared the area below.

A long train of kids about Zach's age and a few adult chaperones trailed to the cement loading dock at the opposite end of the swimming area. Uniformed state park employees herded the groups carefully onto jungle cruise boats. One by one, the boats left the dock and inched upriver. I heard bits and pieces of their nature lessons over the boats' speakers. After a slow circle around the deep mouth of the spring, the motors roared to life, sending a wake into the swimming area.

Aunt Neece looked up from her mystery novel. "I suppose you kids will want to take one of those water tours."

I dug my toes into the sand and shrugged. "I'm good without it." My brother and I had spent hours on the rivers and lakes with our parents, so it didn't much appeal to me. I'd rather use my time sketching. I looked toward the dive platform. I knew where Zach would rather fritter away his day—part flying fish, part annoying little brother.

At two o'clock, the wind stirred the feathery cypress canopy. A low grumble like the engine of a barge sounded in the distance. Aunt Neece lowered her novel. No ominous clouds marred the perfect sky, but the thick trees could cover an approaching storm until it was on top of us. She fished her smartphone from a waterproof sack and used the Weather Channel app to check the area radar.

"Got a few pop-up squalls here and there. I could set a clock on the storms this time of year." She pivoted her head to glance at the dive platform. Other than the thirty-minute break Aunt Neece had imposed after our lunch, Zach had kept up a continuous climb and jump, climb and jump. I know what my great aunt was thinking: if we could wear him out and keep him away from any more sugar, we stood a chance of enjoying a calm afternoon and evening.

Or at least Aunt Neece would. My night, if it rained, might be very unquiet.

"We'd best take one more dip in the springs and then dry off," Aunt Neece said. "Won't be long before we have to pack up."

Springs in Florida stay a constant 72° even in the winter, but each time my big toe touched the water, it felt more like a deep freeze. I couldn't plunge in like Zach. For sure, my heart would stall. I inched in, allowing the skin to numb out before wading farther. Aunt Neece worked her way in beside me, holding her arms and shoulders high, making hissing noises every time she moved.

We were only waist-deep when a waving line caught my eye. It moved toward the shallow water. Nope, it wasn't a piece of eelgrass, but a foot-long snake. Desperate to flee the clamor of humans, it popped to the surface long enough to breathe before diving and swimming. I knew what most of the non-venomous water snakes looked like. Gray or brownish. This one had coppery stripes like a cottonmouth moccasin, a type known for both venom and aggressiveness, but it swam with its head beneath the water, so probably not. No need to freak.

Keeping the snake in sight, I set a route parallel and moved faster. The kid with the pail played a few feet ahead. When I reached the little boy, I leaned down and said in a calm voice, "Let's go to the bank, okay? A little creature is trying to swim by."

He looked up at me, then stood up and headed for a woman sitting in a chair near the water's edge. She lowered her sunglasses to study me.

"A water snake," I said. "Nothing to be afraid of. It's trying to reach the other side of the dive platform."

The woman jumped up, grabbed her son, and yelled to a man sleeping on a lounge chair beneath a tree. A crowd of excited people gathered, herding the snake.

"It's okay. Really!" I called out. "It just wants to be left alone."

Lucky for the snake, the cypress trees on the other side of the dive platform provided perfect cover. In less time than it took me to return to where Aunt Neece stood, the excitement had passed.

"What was that all about?" she asked.

"Oh, nothing. Little snake."

I wondered why I felt the need to make everyone else *think* it was harmless when I wasn't truly positive. I knew the answer. They'd try to kill it.

Aunt Neece mumbled something about serpents and good energy. Before I could ask, she said, "Lots of creatures down here. An alligator long as me lives across the river. No telling how many snakes are within feet of where we are right now. That's Florida for you."

I nodded.

Aunt Neece pointed to the gathering of people leaning over the dock's railing. "We should go out to the floating dock and watch the manatees. But first, on the count of three... one, two... three!" She plunged under. I couldn't let her show me up, so I did too.

I popped my head from the cold water and squealed. Aunt Neece flipped her mop of red hair back and water shot over her in an arc. I noticed a half-inch, crescent-shaped reddish-brown line behind her left ear at the hairline. "Hey, you have the same birthmark I do!" I whipped my wet hair to one side and turned so she could see.

She offered only a slight nod in reply. "C'mon. Race you to the dock." Before I could say anything, she plunged forward. I tore out a couple of strokes behind her. We reached the floating platform at almost the same time.

"Tie, I'd say." She laughed and climbed up the three-rung metal ladder. We sat on the edge with our legs dangling in the water and watched two manatees—a cow and her calf—bob beneath the surface. Periodically, one of their snouts broke the surface and they snuffled air before sinking back down. I glanced at Aunt Neece, waiting for her to launch into a teachable moment, but she didn't. When she noticed me looking her way, she reached up and rearranged her hair to cover the birthmark.

I turned to search the dive platform for Zach and spotted him, positioned on the top tier. The lifeguard lowered his hand, and my brother sailed, headfirst, into the spring. Aunt Neece grunted beside me. Oh boy. Zach was so busted!

"Not a word, Aidan. Let me handle your brother."

The rain came on schedule. Before the first big drops, we carted our gear to the shelter of the bathhouses. At one point, lightning struck so close, I didn't have time to count between it and the thunder. The smell of ozone mixed with rain. Good thing we weren't by the water. My protective talisman, J's scale tip, rested in my swimsuit cover-up pocket.

When the storm showed no sign of clearing, the lifeguards blew their whistles and waved their arms. "People! We're closing up for the day."

Zach moaned and groaned. We packed up, then moved to the lodge's porch to sit and drip dry. Once the leading edge of the storm passed and the thunder sounded farther upriver, we scurried to the car and headed toward Tallahassee.

"Zach, do you have anything to tell me?" Aunt Neece glanced from the road to the rearview mirror, then back.

My little brother looked like he wanted to claw his way from the back seat and land on the road. Anything to avoid having to 'fess up.

"What was the one thing I asked you not to do today?" She asked.

"Dive."

"And what did you do, sir?"

"Dive, but just once."

"At least you owned it. I detest lying." She paused for a moment. What kind of torment would Zach have to endure for breaking this, not only a Camp Neece rule, but a Safety Rule? I had scrubbed three toilets for my tiny pale lies, even if the punishment had been of my own making. A Safety Rule violation might cause a person to sweep the entire block's sidewalks or tune up the car or lick the cat box clean with his tongue. Eww!

"Zach, tonight you will cook *and* serve *and* clean up after dinner," Aunt Neece announced.

My stomach lurched. No telling what that dinner would be. Hot dogs, dry with just buns. Soggy picnic leftover peanut butter and jelly sandwiches. My evil, delinquent brother had spoiled our last night at Camp Neece. I fired him the stink-eye to end all stink-eyes.

Zach carried on like he had been covered in honey and stuffed into an ant bed as soon as he stepped into the kitchen. He stomped around, making faces and whimpering about how he shouldn't have to do everything by himself.

"Cut the dramatics." Aunt Neece stood near the sink with her arms crossed over her chest. "I won't abide shortcuts. No ordinary spaghetti sauce from a jar. Nope, this will be red sauce from scratch."

I watched from my reporter's seat at the oak table, ready to take notes and ask questions to make sure I recorded the recipe correctly. I glanced at Grandmother Ivey's watch, the one Charity admired so much. Nothing I could do about her at this moment.

First, Aunt Neece browned the ground turkey meat. Good move. No need to let Zach burn down the house. But she gave him the wooden spatula so he could sauté the chopped onions. Not a good move. He whipped the utensil in wild circles. Onions sailed in every direction.

"Watch what you're doing, son!" Aunt Neece clamped her hand over his. Mr. Pig twirled below, waiting for something edible to land. He sniffed a hunk of hot onion and backed off.

"Why can't Aidan do *some*thing?" Zach whined.

"She didn't dive off the platform. You did."

Zach shot me a dark look. I mimed *nannie-nannie-boo-boo*. Bet Charity was glad she didn't have a little brother. But she did have a lost sister. I checked my watch.

My aunt took lead on preparing the sauce, instructing Zach to add ingredients to the pot while she stirred. "There," she said when all the ingredients had been combined in the big pot. She turned down the burner and put a lid on the pot. "That's got to simmer a little. Aidan, please help your brother wipe up this mess. Then you two go play on the computer. I'm taking a little nap."

When the meal was ready, Zach puffed up like he was the greatest Italian chef this side of the globe, the universe, the entire Milky Way. Zach the Magnifico.

Aunt Neece grabbed her smartphone and snapped a picture of the master cook standing in front of the stove with the dishrag draped over one shoulder, then one of him posing before the table pointing to the beautiful meal he had prepared. Red blotches stood out across the front of his chef's apron like he'd been in a paintball war using ripe tomatoes.

"This is the best, the most fantastic, the *wonderfulest* spaghetti ever!" Zach crammed a twirled forkful of pasta into his mouth and slurped up one hanging strand.

"*Wonderfulest* is not a word," I pointed out.

"Is too." He wiggled his tongue at me. His lips glistened orange with tomato sauce.

Even I had to admit he had done a super-fine job. He had even eaten ground turkey meat instead of beef... and onions! Amazement upon amazement.

Zach's complaining started anew when he had to wash the dishes. "The pasta sticks everywhere! My fingers are turning into prunes! I hate to scrub yucky pots!"

Aunt Neece and I lounged at the table with our glasses of ice water and exchanged snorty sighs each time he erupted with a new gripe. At that point, who was being punished?

My aunt's lips drew into the straight-line thing she does when she's *done, done, done*.

"One more peep," she said, "one more teeny-tiny freep, and you'll be heading for bed before the sun goes down, young man."

Good call, Aunt Neece. We'd be traveling to the midway point to meet Mama and Daddy for the trip home to Lake City, first thing the next morning. Four days had passed by so fast. One last night at Camp Neece. I gazed from one of the long windows by the table nook. The dreary skies promised rain. Hope so. It would be the last time to open the Rainy Day Box. Last time to help Charity. If Zach had to hit the bed early, I'd just go without him. *By myself*. My heart beat a little faster.

Zach finished scrubbing the pots in relative silence. His left foot tapped a complex rhythm: his irritation indicator. I glanced at my mood bracelet to see if it had turned a new color. A confused greyish—guess it didn't have a special shade for gloating because your little brother got his just rewards. Maybe it should've been orange since I felt more edgy by the second.

Aunt Neece mixed the few noodles with sauce and placed them in a burp-seal container in the refrigerator. "For later, when one of you gets the nibbles. And I know you will."

Zach shot me a look and I knew exactly what he was thinking. Leftovers! That crazy sushi-eating dragon "absolutely and completely adored" spaghetti sauce.

I wasn't the only one hoping to open the box one last time before we left Camp Neece.

I needed to help Charity. Without Zach, of course.

CHAPTER ELEVEN

No rain! I tossed and turned until the sheet wrapped around me like a boa constrictor. I wrestled from its clutches and inched from the airbed to glance over the edge of the double pedestal bed where Zach slept. That's how it went at Camp Neece. Zach got the bed. I got the air mattress on the floor, but it wasn't so bad.

The digital clock on the bedside table read 11:30 p.m. in glowing red numerals. I could barely hear the low rumble of the television from the living room. Sugar! No rain *and* Aunt Neece was still awake. Now, on the final night of Camp Neece, my last chance to visit the Rainy Day Box and help Charity, the sky had decided to dry up.

I huffed and flopped back into the airbed. My stomach growled. That leftover spaghetti would be good right about now, but the 9 p.m. official kitchen off-limits deadline had passed two and a half hours ago. While I mulled over the events of the past three days, sleep snuck up and took me out.

A boom of thunder jerked me from a sinister dream where something big and dark chased me. For a moment, I didn't know if the sound had leached from my nightmare, or if it was real. Lightning flashed through the window blinds and rain thrummed the roof, followed by more thunder. Nope, real for sure. I sat upright and squinted into the low light to where Zach lay. He hadn't moved a single toe. One thing about my brother, he slept like a rock once he stopped long enough to become still. A dump truck could rumble across the room and he would snooze through it.

"Now or never, Aidan," I encouraged myself in a whisper. I flipped back the sheet and tiptoed from the bedroom, hugging the wall so the old wooden stairs and floor wouldn't creak. At the threshold to the living room, I paused and peeked around the corner. Aunt Neece sprawled in her easy chair with her mouth wide open. I leaned forward and listened. Either she wasn't snoring, or I couldn't hear her snores over the noise of the storm.

I crouched down and slid into the room at floor level. Mr. Pig spotted me and trilled. I held one finger to my lips. "Shhh!" He jumped down from his spot on Aunt Neece's lap, did a long cat-yoga stretch and ambled over to where I cowered. Sissy slipped up behind me and touched her cold nose to the bottom of one of my feet and I nearly squealed. Good thing Aunt Neece didn't have barking dogs. I'd be busted, for sure.

Other than the strobe of the television, no lights illuminated the room. Some random station played an old Godzilla movie instead of the usual Weather Channel. Very bizarre. The Doppler Radar picture was *always* on, with red, green, and yellow blobs to show the storm cells in the area. Something was very wrong. Aunt Neece had been so tired and acting not herself. Now this. Fear gripped me and my chest squeezed. Other than the times she watched Her Show, since when did my aunt *not* tune into the forecast during storm season? Since never!

I inched toward her chair on my hands and knees, scared as much by the pounding thunder as by the thought she might be sick or... No! I forced the thought from my head. Aunt Neece was pretty old, sure, at least fifty, but not *that* old. But then, she had some kind of thing a couple of years ago, the only summer Zach and I had missed coming to Camp Neece. That was the reason she now worked from home. What if ...

Wish Mama was here. She'd know all the right nurse stuff.

What to do. What to do? I remembered bits and pieces of the First Aid and CPR class I had taken before I started baby sitting at the beginning of summer. Should I dial 911? No, wait. Check for a response; that was the first step. I sat back on my heels. If I did that, I'd have to shake her and yell out her name. Fine, if she wasn't okay—but if she was only sleeping, I'd scare her into a heart attack for sure.

I reached out one shaky hand toward her shoulder, then jerked it back.

But wait! If I woke her up and she was okay and I didn't need to call 911, then she'd wonder why I was out of bed and send me back. I wouldn't be able to help Charity. My head spun with all the possibilities. They didn't cover this scenario in the CPR class.

I inched even closer and leaned in. Her chest rose and fell. Oh, thank goodness! How did you spend your summer vacation, Aidan? I ate sushi with a dragon, tried to help a homeless fairy with a bad attitude, and nearly found my aunt all, like, not alive. I couldn't even make myself think the *d* word.

Aunt Neece honked out a loud snore. I jumped so hard, I nearly fell over. Mr. Pig and Sissy took off down the hall like a demon chased them. Then I got tickled, the way I do sometimes in church when something is totally absurd and I can't laugh right then. I clamped my hand over my mouth and crab-hobbled as fast and soundlessly as I could manage until I reached the far end of the hall. Only then did I give myself over to a case of the full-on shaking giggles.

I let out a low snort and pondered. Zach slept. Aunt Neece snored. It was still raining. I assessed the situation, then made the right choice and went back to our bedroom to make preparations.

Since Aunt Neece sometimes peeked in to check on us, I punched my pillow into a me-shaped lump and covered it with the sheet, stuffing it in places to look like a sleeping person. I pulled on my shorts and shirt and felt to make sure the triangle of J's scale still rested in one pocket. I groped around in the dark and put a hand down on my running shoes but found only one sock. What else? I thought of the sinister place Charity lived. I bumped my way to the nightstand and eased out the single drawer to find a small flashlight. Aunt Neece believed in keeping one near each bed in case the power went out. I attached its clip to a belt loop on my shorts, then ran my fingers across the top of the bureau. Mood bracelet. Grandmother Ivey's watch. Check. I slipped both on and crammed the San Luis Mission T-shirt in its gift bag into my side cargo pocket.

"Always stop to think," Mama often reminded me. "The devil is in the details." I wasn't real sure what that meant, but in this case, probably something about double-checking before you headed into a situation that included dragons and giant rats. I padded down the hall, through the living room, and into the kitchen. A tiny chicken-shaped plug-in cast enough light to help me find a notepad and pen in the junk drawer next to the stove.

Gone to help a friend, I wrote. *11:45 p.m.* I fastened the note on the front of the refrigerator with a Mickey Mouse magnet. Every time Mama and I went dragonfly hunting, we left a note in the car with the date and time we entered the woods.

In case we didn't come out.

I shivered at that thought, took one quick look back into the house, then slipped into the sunroom.

The Rainy Day Box drew me in the same way moths flocked to our back porch light in the evening. One step, two steps, three, and I stood in front of its pedestal, the cedar chest. I bowed from the waist. It just seemed right. Aidan McAllister, willing servant come to pay homage. Then I felt dumb.

"It's only an old wooden box," I reminded myself.

Maybe I should've awakened Zach. Nope. This way, I'd only have to look after myself. I opened the lid and... nothing happened.

I let out the breath I wasn't aware I had been holding. Mama called this a "pivotal moment," the spot where I had one instant to decide whether or not to take action. The pause puffed with importance and I waited a beat before reaching inside for Charity's touchstone and setting it on the floor.

"Hmm." I stood with my arms propped on my hips, waiting for the dark fairy to swirl from the shadows.

The shard of J's armor vibrated slightly like an anxious caged animal. I put one hand in my pocket and probed for the shard, then stopped. Should I try to wake up the dragon? J and Charity weren't friends. Why add that to the mix? J would clamor for hors d'oeuvres or that leftover spaghetti and I couldn't risk noise in the kitchen—plus time was running out.

Still, my spirit sank. I wouldn't be able to see J for quite some time. With school starting—studying, cheerleading, my writing and art—a long visit in Tallahassee probably wouldn't happen until next summer. If Aunt Neece came to Lake City, she might not bring the Rainy Day Box. I missed that silly dragon already.

But Charity needed my help. And J wouldn't approve of me taking any risks for her. I sighed. If she wasn't coming to me, I'd have to go to her. I put a finger on the stone, closed my eyes, summoned my courage, and whispered the mantra: *Through stone. Through glass. Through time.*

As if it had awaited my firm no-dragon-allowed decision, and the passcode words, the touchstone swelled to twenty times its size. I stood up and backed away. A thick green fog oozed from its surface and curled at my feet. The vapor climbed my body, inching like a famished snake until I felt trapped. Where was Charity? The mist rose to cover my chin, my lips and nose, and my eyes. I smelled the dank filth of the landfill. The sunroom shimmered out of focus, then rippled like the surface of a peaceful pond shattered by a skipped rock.

My eyes were wide open. I could see nothing, but my ears picked up tiny scrabbling noises, squeaks. I shuddered. Bats? Rats? The oppressive odor scorched my nose. My stomach roiled. Good thing I hadn't eaten that leftover spaghetti; it would be making a colorful comeback.

Something brushed against one of my calves. "Sugar!" I shifted my feet. Something bumped against my hip. The flashlight! My fingers wrapped around it and I fumbled with the clasp. With a metallic click, it released from my belt loop. I snapped the switch on. Then I wished I hadn't.

This wasn't like the last time, at the landfill. I was underground somewhere. The thin beam highlighted the walls, floor, and low ceiling of some kind of tunnel. No dragon. No Charity. No rats... so far, but plenty of cockroaches. They didn't scurry from my light. Black and white plastic refuse bags filled the space around me, mixed with soggy cardboard boxes, tattered papers, and soiled disposable diapers. "Ugh!"

The contents of the closest bag poured from a jagged tear: rotten potato peels and something white like bits of animated rice on a piece of graying meat. I leaned forward to figure out what the wiggling things were, then drew back. Maggots. Lots of them. My stomach lurched.

"I will not throw up. I will not throw up!" I repeated. "Even breaths, three in a row, Aidan. Do not think about the disgusting air."

Fly larvae served a purpose, Mama had once assured me. Otherwise, we'd be up to our armpits in dead things. I remembered the time we had stumbled upon a bloated raccoon baking in the summer heat. How it had ruined our dragonfly expedition. "Fact of life, Aidan," Mama said. Sure. But it was a nasty fact of life, or death.

The thought of my protective mother made my knees weak, and desolation washed over me. Why hadn't I brought J with me? But he'd be too big to fit in here. Even my little brother would've been welcome.

The spot where I stood appeared to be a blind alley, the bulbous end of a long tunnel. Either I had to ditch the idea of helping Charity, wherever the heck she was, or press on. If *my* brother was lost and *I* lived in a dump, I'd hope for a friend with courage, one who wouldn't duck and run.

Resolve cemented inside. I bent down and rested one hand on the touchstone and imagined holding it in my palm. It worked. The boulder shriveled and I pocketed it with the dragon scale shard. As long as I had the touchstone, I could go home anytime I pleased, right? It had brought Charity here last time, then sent us back to the sunroom. And she probably used it to show up at the museum too. Surely it would work again for me. It just had to.

The narrow alley opened into a long subway formed by bulging trash walls, paved with garbage. I hummed to take my mind from where I had landed. The only tune that popped into my brain was "hot dog, hot dog, hot diggety dog" from the Mickey Mouse Clubhouse, my baby cousin's favorite show. What was up with that? Shades of Babysitting 101. At least it shoved aside the scary thoughts freezing me in place. I forced my feet to move. One step. Another. Until I moved at an even pace.

The single tunnel wove through the garbage walls. After ten or twelve turns, a dim light shone in the distance. The shaft I had been following veered to the left. The one with the light, a narrower passage, cut to the right. Too many switchbacks, and I'd never find my way back to where I had started. The place reminded me of a corn maze my family had visited one fall—a complicated labyrinth with a gazillion ways to go.

Mark the path, my inner voice whispered. I tore off a swatch of the bright yellow Mission San Luis gift bag and crammed it between two dingy white trash bags at the corner. Wasn't a fantastic waypoint, marking a trash wall with more trash, but it was all I had. The flashlight beam flickered then went out.

"NO!" I shook it hard. The light shone steadily again. I took a raspy breath and turned right, following the narrow path. My shoes slipped on something squishy. I didn't bother to shine the light to see what had wedged itself into the tread of my running shoes. In a few feet, I rounded a slight bend and halted.

This place appeared different from the tunnels. A ripped blue tarp formed a tent against one wall and several intact boxes looked as if they might serve as tables and storage. Something, or someone, lived here.

"Who are you?" A gravelly voice demanded.

I jerked and spun around, shining my meager light in the direction of the voice. A dwarfish man stood behind me, his red knuckles propped on his hips.

The little man was one big wrinkle. His jacket, pants, face, skin, hair, and beard would take hours' worth of ironing to look normal, and only after a good bath.

"I... I... Aidan," I managed.

"Aye-Aye Aidan. Odd name." He looked me up and down.

"No. Just Aidan."

He pulled on his beard, then thumped his chest with one grime-outlined thumbnail. "I'm Malcolm."

We stood, staring at each other for a beat, then one of his hairy eyebrows cocked up. "Something I might assist you with?"

The way he asked—like I was in a department store and he was there to help me choose the perfect shirt—struck me as funny. I smiled. At least he wasn't evil, or a rat. "I'm looking for someone. Charity."

He made an abrupt noise, a cross between a snort and a harrumph. "The... what does she call herself now? ... fair-a-tude? What do you want with *her*?"

"She needs my help."

"No helping the likes of her." He trundled over to one of the boxes and sat down. "Pull up a seat, Aidan." Malcolm pronounced my name with a lot of *A* and a pinch of *dan:* AAAA-dan. "Best save that." He motioned to my flashlight. "Batteries are hard to come by here, at least ones that have any juice."

A small oil lamp cast an amber glow in a circle. I switched the flashlight off and secured it to the clip on my shorts.

"I'm having tea. Will you join me?" He motioned to a steaming pot atop a one-burner propane stove, the kind my dad used when he and Zach went hunting and spent the night in the woods.

I peered down the passageway extending to a whole lot of nowhere. I glanced at my wrist. The mood bracelet showed a calm blue. How long had I been away from Camp Neece? Twenty minutes, an hour? I strained my eyes to see the time on Grandmother Ivey's watch. The tiny second hand stood still. Great, I'd forgotten to wind it. As long as I returned before the flicker of wake-up lights, all would be good. "I should look for Charity."

"Tea first." Malcolm dug in one of the boxes and extracted two chipped, mismatched china cups. He poured a brown liquid from the battered pot and handed me a cup.

He lifted his cup in a little salute, then drank. I paused for a second before taking a tentative sip. Couldn't be poison if he drank it. It tasted of summer sunshine with a hint of honey. "Yum. What is this?"

"Lemongrass. I have chamomile and Earl Grey if you'd prefer." He waved to the boxes stacked along his compartment. "You'd be amazed at the perfectly good stuff people throw away."

I smiled and he returned the expression. The wrinkles around his eyes and mouth shifted into happy creases. I decided to like Malcolm.

What did you do on your summer vacation, Aidan? I ate sushi with a dragon, almost had to do CPR on my aunt, did my best to help a wayward homeless fairy with an attitude, and sipped honeyed tea with a trash-heap dwarf. Made those theme parks in South Florida sound *so* dullsville.

CHAPTER TWELVE

Malcolm stood with a grunt, then slung a shabby backpack over one shoulder. "Let's go then." He removed a cloth-wrapped stick from a wall brace, lit the end with the oil lamp's flame, then snuffed the wick.

I slugged down the rest of the tea—it was too good to waste—and set the cup beside his in a plastic pan filled with a couple of inches of murky water, probably his version of a sink. "I have no idea where to look for Charity."

"Oh, I'm pretty sure I know." His expression told me he wasn't too pleased. Maybe I should go ahead by myself. The thought chilled me.

I trudged behind him for a while. We took so many turns, I didn't have time to wedge any trail markers into the corners. Some tunnels were wide; others narrowed to the point I had to duck and hold my arms close to my sides—didn't want to touch the walls, that's for sure. None of them smelled good. I didn't turn on my flashlight since Malcolm carried the torch and obviously knew which way to go.

The flickering light cast an orange glow on the garbage walls and I couldn't make out small details like maggots or cockroaches. No problem there. I didn't need to see them to know they existed—I could hear the skitter of tiny legs. Once, a shadowy low thing, definitely a mammal, scurried across one intersection. Malcolm clucked and hissed and the dark lump moved off in another direction.

"Stick close to me," Malcolm warned. "We're coming to the Great Hall."

"You got it." Like I would let him out of my sight. Ahead, a roar of voices echoed in waves. Sounded like a whole lot of somebodies were having one heck of a party. My first instinct: Run! Instead, I took a deep breath, as much putrid air as my lungs could hold, and let it out slowly. "You can do this, Aidan," I said to myself. I *would* do this. Besides, whoever *they* were, the party was in full-gear. Who would notice me and a dwarf?

The tunnel opened up, and I stopped to gape at the wild scene in front of me.

Dragons in every shade of the rainbow made my eyes leak water. And dwarfs like Malcolm yelled out wagers and swilled from bottles and thick crocks.

"What... what?"

"Dragon duel party." Malcolm shifted his pack to the other shoulder. "Act normal and try to blend."

Blend? I could barely breathe.

The vast room reminded me of the council house at Mission San Luis, only ten times larger. Beams fashioned from logs and pieces of metal supported the walls, and a pyre burped thick smoke toward an opening in the center of the ceiling. Tables fashioned from jagged planks of sheetrock and plywood circled the room, filled with platters of food. Dwarfs cooked slabs of meat on long braziers and everyone lined up to snatch up what they could reach. Garbage bags hung like crepe paper streamers from the beams. And the noise! Human voices mingled with what I could only describe as pow! and sizzle sounds—dragons speaking to each other in their own language.

At first, no one noticed our entrance, then a woman in a pale blue gown handed each of us a tepid bottle of frothy brown liquid. I hesitated. I had tasted beer once and didn't like it. Malcolm noticed my expression and motioned for me to lean down. "Drink up, young human. No worries," he said into my ear. "'Tis dragon ale, not alcoholic. They put a halt to that centuries ago, after a fire that nearly laid this place to ruin." He cast his gaze up toward the ceiling. "I remember it like 'twas yesterday." He shook his head. "It was awful, awful. Booze and dragon fire don't mix. Nah, they do not."

Malcolm slugged down the ale, then wiped his mouth and let out a resounding belch. From the riot of sounds around me, landfill dwarfs and dragons had the same rude manners. Malcolm furrowed his brow and nodded toward my bottle. I shrugged, held the rim to my lips, and took a tiny sip. It burned like fire all the way down my throat. I coughed and sputtered. Then the aftertaste hit: a noxious blend of sour apples, slime, and swamp.

"This is seriously nasty," I said in a low voice, trying not to gag.

"You're a cosantóir. You should be used to dragon ale."

"What's a *cousin-toy*?"

"A cosantóir is the guardian of a dragon." The dwarf looked at me with squinty eyes. "And you didn't say it right. It is *cos-un-toy*."

I started to tell him I wasn't a cosantóir, wasn't anyone's guardian, especially a dragon's, but a shadow fell over us. Malcolm blinked his pale eyes.

My gaze took in rows of belly scales, bright scarlet tinged with yellow tips. I gasped, then looked up. Two eyes that blazed like twin bonfires regarded me. The head lowered until those eyes were inches from mine. This dragon's breath made J's seem like roses in comparison. I breathed through my mouth to give my nose a break.

"Where is your dragon, little cosantóir?" it asked in a low gurgle.

I turned fast, but Malcolm had deserted me. I saw him wiggle his fingers my way from nearby. He and another dwarf had settled into an instant conversation, like I wasn't freaking out and in need of his support.

"I've been asking myself that same question." I tried for a casual tone. "Haven't seen that dragon for a while now, not since he had his twelfth ale." I scanned the room, as if my dragon—whoever *that* might be—hung out somewhere in the milling masses.

The scarlet dragon reached one talon toward my head. Everything inside told me to haul buggy, but I stood still. He reached behind my left ear and gently lifted my hair to examine my birthmark. Then he made the same rumble noise deep in his throat J made when he was amused or pleased.

"Ah, you're here with J." He lifted his huge head and swung it in both directions. "Haven't seen him, but he's probably with the group from Japan. One of their cosantóirs is making fresh lobster rolls."

"Um... yep. That would be about right." I forced my lips to turn up. "I do love it when one of my fellow cosantóirs cooks." I kept my fingers crossed I had pronounced it right this time: *cos-un-toys.*

"Move along then, little guardian." A hot breeze brushed my face when he stepped aside.

I let out the breath I'd been holding, nodded, and plowed into the crowd, no clue as to where I was supposed to head.

Any direction that made me look like I knew where I was going would do. Malcolm reappeared and fell into step beside me.

"Thanks for the back-up, Malcolm."

"No choice on that, Aidan. Dragons only speak with each other before duels, and to guardians and their kin. That's a hard fast rule. If I had butted in, someone might question your authority."

But I didn't have any authority and I didn't know the rules. I had no business here.

That certainty caught up with my brain at the same instant I spied Charity through the crowd. She stood beside a girl slightly smaller in size, one with white-blonde hair and silver wings. I picked up the pace, dodging dragons in every hue, and bumping into humans of all ages, shapes, and sizes. Some scolded me in foreign words, others just glowered and moved from my path.

"Charity!" I called out as soon as I drew close enough.

She swung her head in my direction. When she spotted me, she scowled. My heart sank. She should be running up, all happy to see me. After all, I had trudged through acres of scummy trash to find her.

"What are you doing here?" Charity took a step away from the other fairy and stood rigid. Resentment boiled from her in shimmers.

"I... I'm here to help you find your sister." My voice came out a little squeaky.

Malcolm stood by my side, looking from one of us to the other like he was watching a tennis match.

Charity huffed and jabbed her hands onto her hips. The crowd of guardians and dragons around her halted their conversations and tuned in. My excitement at finding her dimmed even more. Our little drama had become the moment's entertainment.

"My *sister*?" The laugh that came from her held no mirth, only mockery. "My sister isn't lost."

"Wait, that's her, isn't it?" I pointed to the fair girl beside her. "Faith, right?"

The two of them exchanged glances and broke into deep belly laughs.

"Yeah, so okay, Faith is *one* of my sisters. Hope's the other one. You don't even want to meet her. Hope is unbalanced, like, *way* beyond unbalanced." She chuckled again, and the circle of onlookers laughed with her.

I noticed Charity's outfit: a clean gray shirt with new jeans. No dirt marred her face. Her hair—no longer cropped, but long and flowing—appeared washed and she'd pulled it back into a loose ponytail. No grime ringed her neck. Her fingernails were manicured, painted pale pink. No flip-flops on her feet. Instead, black high-heeled boots. And she didn't look as if it had been months since her last decent meal.

Something didn't add up. A lot of things didn't add up. I knew from her malevolent gaze: I was in the hot seat at this festive little party. Had she known I would show up?

I unsnapped the pocket in my cargo shorts. "I must have misunderstood. My bad." I held the gift bag toward her. "I brought you this."

Charity's face flickered with shock before she brought it under control and back to irritated indifference. She tore into the bag and unfurled the T-shirt. For a second, I wondered if she might cry. Then she wiped the sentiment from her face and held up the shirt, circling around the group of onlookers so everyone could see. "Look what *she* brought for *me*."

Most of them chortled. A few huffed. Charity flipped the shirt around and traced her finger around the butterfly design. "Isn't this just..." She pulled a knife blade from her jeans and ripped two long tears down the backside, then slipped it over her gray shirt. She wiggled her dark wings—no longer tattered now, but full and flowing—from the gaps.

She paraded around the circle of dragons, dwarfs, and humans with her arms flung wide. I took my eyes off her long enough to throw a questioning look toward Malcolm. He shook his head slightly and formed the word *no* with his lips.

Who was this person, er, fair-a-tude? And why did everyone in the hall kowtow to her as if they admired her every move?

She ended her one-fairy parade. "My dragon," Charity said with her chest puffed out, "is going to take one look at this stupid shirt and laugh his black scales off." The corners of her lips lifted, but the smile didn't make it to her dark eyes.

"Then," she stepped to within inches of where I stood and leaned in so close I could smell her fetid breath, "he's going to destroy you."

Betrayal. I had experienced the feeling before—some silly, mean-girls showdown at school. But nothing like this.

Fear sucked every speck of water from my mouth. I was going to die in a landfill and I'd never see my family or friends again. Ever. My spirit ached. If I could touch my heart, it might shatter into splinters so tiny, they would disintegrate to dust and disappear into the cracks in the landfill walls.

Malcolm brushed my arm with his hand. I glanced down at him. He pulled himself to his full height—standing straight, he came up to my waist—and squared his shoulders. I looked away from Malcolm to the petite blonde fairy. I couldn't read her face at all. When she wasn't mirroring Charity, her features were washed clean, like those rich ladies on television who needled Botox into their faces to smooth their skin.

The air crackled with the snap from the bonfire, and with the expectant energy from the crowd. Bravery had buried itself in my deepest cells, but I managed to suck up my courage.

"So what, Charity..." I forced out a clipped laugh and gestured to the fire pit. "What cha going to do, roast me over the hot coals because I bought you a *shirt*?" I spun around and addressed the crowd. "You people know how to have a good time. I mean, insult a fellow guardian... really?"

The humans in the group exchanged worried glances. Bingo! I noticed some whispering to others, probably translating my English to whatever tongue they spoke. The dragons took it in like they understood every word. Did they know as many languages as J?

I warmed to my act. "And how will *my* dragon feel about that, huh?" The edges of the circle broke apart, as if my words had provided a wedge in their good time.

Charity's head swiveled, right then left. She narrowed her ebony eyes and tilted her head. "But you're *not* a cosantóir, are you Aidan?" When she spoke my name, her teeth showed.

The crowd reformed and more joined the edges. The air felt suddenly thick, the light dimmer.

Charity turned three times in a tight circle then extended her wings. If I hadn't been horrified to my center, I would've been impressed. No Halloween costume could match those wings. They stretched five feet on either side of her shoulders and unfurled with a crisp snap, slick black with red veins radiating and pulsing as the blood coursed through them. As she spun, she rubbed the pendant hanging from her neck chain. The Letter *C*.

Thick acrid smoke scented the air like burning rubber. It boiled up behind Charity in curdled waves. A shadow loomed above the tips of her curved wings.

The crowd inched back. I turned fast, looking for Malcolm, but Charity and I now stood alone in the middle of a circle of intent watchers.

Fire and smoke billowed. When the air cleared, the towering column of smoke became an ebony dragon, dark as a cave buried deep beneath the earth with no chance of daylight. The creature was midnight without stars, as if its scales sucked all the radiance from the room and reflected none back. The only things glittering were its eyes: two huge silver marbles with dark pupil slits, set deep in its bony head. Two long horns snaked out above the eye sockets, their tips pointed downward.

Bits of stored information on this most feared of dragon shades came to me in whispered thoughts. How ebony dragons were evil and obsessed with death. Their hearts were as black as their scales. Their saliva was acidic, caustic. No need to recall the part about its smell; thick air poisoned with rot oozed from the haze around the dragon.

The Mission San Luis T-shirt with its frilly butterflies and innocent sky blue background mocked me. Charity shifted one wing to shield the blonde fairy, the way I pushed Zach behind me when I sensed danger. For a flicker, raw fear shone from Charity's eyes. Then she cloaked that emotion. Once again, Charity played the ebony dragon's evil empress.

The dragon shard vibrated in my cargo pocket. A wispy thought formed in my terror-numbed brain. I acted before I had a chance to rationalize it away.

I raised one hand and mimed an enthusiastic wave, as if I had spotted a long lost, dear friend in the distant crowd. Everyone's attention—including the ebony dragon's—shifted to where I directed. I slipped the other hand into my cargo shorts pocket, grabbed the scale shard, and pushed a wish, a demand, a desire, outward with every mental muscle I possessed.

CHAPTER THIRTEEN

A fierce roar echoed from every direction at once, as if it was piped in over a ginormous loudspeaker. The fine hairs on the back of my neck stood up. I tried to swallow, to lick my parched lips, but my mouth was too dry. All eyes—human, dragon, and dwarf—shifted from the ebony dragon and its fairy consort to the glowing green cloud roiling through the hole above the central fire.

Several things happened at once. A cheer sounded from the crowd. The dragon spectators flapped their wings open and shut like a rainbow of flags in a stiff breeze. Four scale-covered claws appeared, talons extended, then the body and finally the head of a green dragon.

Relief poured over me in a cool waterfall. "J!"

J circled the Great Hall, his massive wings creating a wind so fierce, my hair blew straight back and I struggled to maintain my balance. He landed beside me and slightly in front. His serpentine tail curled around my feet and legs, forming a protective wall—now I was the little kid, like Zach. J glanced down; one green eyelid winked, then he swung his head to face the ebony dragon.

A conversation started between the two goliaths, low and rumbling like semi-trucks revving their engines. The ebony dragon stood a couple of feet taller than J, but J appeared more solid, heavier. Those extra Swiss cake rolls might've been a good thing, as long as J didn't have to out-fly the ebony dragon. And J looked twice as ticked-off as the dark dragon. That had to work in our favor.

Smoke looped from J's mouth and nostrils. I lifted my nose into the air and caught the now-familiar aroma of J, still unpleasant but a perfume compared to that of Charity's defender.

The air to my right shimmered and went out of focus. Aunt Neece and Zach materialized—Zach in his PJs and Aunt Neece in the crumpled outfit she'd fallen asleep in. Why were they here? Unless the force of that green dragon had curved around them too, dragging them in its wake. Both looked dazed. Zach lunged over J's curved tail and grabbed me so hard, I nearly toppled over. Oh no! If J couldn't save us, my aunt and brother would surely die in this dingy place too, thanks to me.

Aunt Neece stood rigid, her face painted with fear. She should be coming to us, opening up her arms, gathering me and Zach in a smothery hug, but she was frozen in place. The mindless terror wafting from her scared me more than the scene unfolding in the Great Hall. Finally, she moved one hand, grasping the other to turn the silver ring on her middle finger around and around. Aunt Neece was losing it, and I couldn't help her either. I tightened my grip on Zach.

The ebony dragon flipped back its head and emitted a high-pitched whistle through its nose. Humans and dwarfs slapped their hands over their ears. The ebony dragon unfurled its wings and lifted off. A shiver shook J's curled tail, then he straightened it carefully without disturbing us, unfolded his wings and shot straight up.

The two dragons circled the massive hall clockwise in positions directly across from one another. Their heads turned to watch each other, neither taking eyes off their adversary. Instead of going all scared spitless like Aunt Neece, Zach, and me, the crowd clapped and cheered. Each time either J or the ebony dragon passed overhead or dipped a wing, the spectators answered with cheers and jeers, like a pep rally before one of my school's football games.

The ebony dragon slung its head and another of those sharp piercing whistles cut the air. My eardrums felt like they would burst. The dark dragon charged, all four legs tucked until the final moment when it extended razor talons. J executed a quick turn and met the ebony dragon in the middle of the aerial arena. Horrific screams and thunder sounded. Wings flapped. Talons slashed. Shards of green and black scales rained down like volcanic ash.

A green liquid squirted into the air and splashed. Dragon blood.

"Move, move, move!" Someone shouted. Humans and dwarfs dove to avoid the caustic blood bath, but I couldn't get my feet to work. Which dragon had been wounded? Not J. Please not J! I strained to make sense of the confusion of wings and fury.

J broke away first. His left wing ruffled in tatters and a long gaping gash glinted on his underbelly. One side of the Great Hall erupted into cheers. The other booed and hissed. I gasped and clapped my hand over my mouth. My mood bracelet jangled against Grandmother Ivey's watch on my wrist, a murky shade of midnight.

J and the ebony dragon circled again, as they had in the beginning. J's torn wing caused him to falter, but he still managed to fly. They dipped, changed directions, dove, and zipped right and left, to the delight of the onlookers. Where had I seen this type of display before? Dragonflies! Of course. The Odes flew in the same haphazard fashion, masters of escape and mid-air trickery. I caught Malcolm peering from beneath a rock table. The dwarf gave a troubled shake of his head.

The ebony dragon banked right and whipped by J. As they passed, one black claw dragged across J's uninjured wing. The ripping noise made my stomach lurch. J managed somehow to maintain altitude but appeared to have trouble maneuvering. His path jogged to one side, then to the other, like a seagull tossed by a gale.

Oh, sugar! J was losing. He hated violence and would die because I was stupid enough to come here. And Aunt Neece, Zach and I would die too. Terror squeezed my chest so hard, my breath puffed out fast and shallow. Zach had not let up on his grip around my waist, but I grasped him even tighter until it felt like we were one person. The crowd's roar increased in volume and I wanted to cry out too. A sea of upraised arms motioned toward a point far from where we stood.

A third dragon had appeared from the murky fog and a blast of intense super-heated wind seared my cheeks. At first, the newcomer appeared as dark as the ebony dragon, until it passed overhead and I could see its true color: deep, mahogany brown. I glanced at Aunt Neece. She still hadn't moved, her face fixed in the same horrified expression.

As I watched, the space beside Aunt Neece shimmered. A figure appeared. The ambling walk, the bird-head cane—Miz Bridie! She acknowledged us with a small nod and wink, and a wicked knowing smile. She lifted her cane and the tip of the carved bird's head glowed crimson. Miz Bridie tilted back her head and let out a trilling yodel. The crowd rippled with cheers and boos. The mahogany dragon dipped its head and one wing our way, then turned on the ebony dragon. The identity of the mahogany dragon struck me. She was even more magnificent in reality than she had been as the carved morph atop Miz Bridie's desk!

The three dragons circled, clashed, circled, tangled again. Green slashing black, brown sinking talons into black, all three meeting in a spinning mass. I expected flames to fly from the dueling trio overhead. The legends always talked about dragon fire. How much better to fry your opponent than all the trick flying and slashing claws!

The battle whipped the crowd around me into a frenzy. Guardians fainted and their dragons dragged them to the periphery of the circle to avoid stamping feet. Around the Great Hall, dragons tilted their heads and called out in screams and snorts. I could pick out J's individual fishy scent in the scalded wind, over the choking odor of spilled blood, decay, and fumes.

When would it end? And how? Miz Bridie seemed more enthralled than anything. Aunt Neece's face remained pale and blank. Zach still hung around my waist, but even he acted as if he was watching the best crash and burn movie scene ever.

The atmosphere shifted again. The light turned yellowish. The fire in the middle of the room shrunk down to smoldering coals. Humans, dwarfs, and dragons glanced around, nervous. Was some other creature going to pop from out of nowhere?

Clumps of onlookers shimmered and disappeared. Dwarfs scattered like sprayed cockroaches. Malcolm shot me a nod, then he too scurried and dove into the passageway where he and I had first entered the Great Hall.

The ebony dragon shoved back from the fray and swooped low to pick up Charity by the shoulders. One moment, I saw her hanging in mid-air with a pained expression as she reached feebly for the blonde fairy. The next, the dragon and Charity dissolved into nothingness. The blonde fairy stared at the spot for a beat, then went out of focus and evaporated.

The brown dragon swept down and scooped up Miz Bridie with one extended claw. "Good luck and dragon speed to you!" Miz Bridie called out. I heard her raucous laughter as her red lace-up shoes left the ground—and then—they weren't there.

J landed beside the three of us with a thud. His damaged left wing luffed like a shredded mainsail. He gathered Aunt Neece, Zach, and me with the other wing. He sneered at the remaining onlookers surrounding us and grumbled something in dragon-speak.

I thought I heard him say, "This party's over." His words dissolved as fast as the chaotic image of the Great Hall.

Aunt Neece, Zach, and I appeared in the sunroom, still in a clump. Aunt Neece hugged us so hard, we made choking noises. She rocked us back and forth like she was scared to let go. Mr. Pig yawned and stretched on the rocker, then regarded us with sleepy eyes. The Rainy Day Box, closed now with its Happy Meal sword, secrets, and a silent dragon, sat on the cedar chest. Just an ordinary wooden box.

Outside, crickets sang. The neighborhood steamed, rinsed clean by the passing storm. No traffic noises, no sound of children playing. The lonesome call of a howling dog sounded in the distance. The night train whistle blew—a forlorn wail that made me ache deep in my chest.

"It's late." Aunt Neece released her hold and pushed back from our tangle of arms. "To bed with you both."

Questions tumbled around in my brain, stepping on each other. “But—”

She rested one palm on my head, then stroked my hair the same way she petted Mr. Pig or Sissy. “Go to bed, Aidan,” Aunt Neece said. Her voice sounded old, tired. She put one arm around me, gave my shoulder a gentle squeeze, then turned me toward the stairs. “Tomorrow is a full day. We have to get up in a few hours. Have breakfast. Drive to meet your parents.”

Zach yawned and stretched. He shuffled from the sunroom. What was going on? The little dude who normally bounced around like an electrified pogo stick headed back to bed without a word, and after witnessing the dragon battle of the century? Could it be that Zach didn’t remember any of it?

My nerves jittered. One moment, death and dragons and dread. The next, off to sweet dreams. Was I the only one freaking out a little here?

CHAPTER FOURTEEN

After Zach crawled into the pedestal bed and Aunt Neece turned out the light, he zonked out. I closed my eyes and tried to will myself to sleep, but the bloody fight scene played in my head. I gave up and retrieved my aunt's small flashlight and my sketchbook and pencils from my quilted tote bag—now packed for the trip home—and drew and drew. The tunnels. The maggoty meat. Malcolm holding his tea cup. The Great Hall. Charity and the blonde fairy with the ebony dragon. Miz Bridie and the brown dragon. J's ripped wings.

I added shading and tinted highlights: the green liquid gushing from J's belly wound, the ebony dragon's silver eyes with their dark slits, the rainbow colors of the dragons and their jeering guardians. Too bad Aunt Neece had gone all wonky. She could've taken photos with the smartphone she always kept clamped to her belt. But even if she had tried, who would believe that scene, even with pictures? And for sure, we couldn't message the images off to Mama and Daddy.

At some point, I dozed off, a colored pencil in hand.

The overhead light flicked on and off, on and off, but more slowly than usual. "Time to get up, kiddos." Aunt Neece's voice didn't come out in a song, like it usually did first thing in the morning. I wiped the sleep crust from my eyes.

I patted the sheets for my pad and pencils and found them neatly packed in my tote bag. I flipped to the pages at the back—looking for my drawings of the dragon battle, the landfill. Nothing but blank paper! No drawings after the ones I had sketched at Wakulla Springs. I snapped the pad shut and shoved it back into my bag. Did I dream I had set those awful images to paper? I held my forearm to my nose. Shouldn't the stench from that place linger on my skin and clothing? Nothing.

Zach rolled onto his stomach, stuck out his feet from beneath the covers, and slid backwards from bed until his feet hit the floor. He shuffled to the hall bathroom, his eyes barely held open to slits. I heard the sharp opening whap of the toilet seat, and Mr. Pig conversing with him in loud piteous yowls. Sissy poked her head from a spot beneath my sheet and bumped my hand. I stroked under her chin.

Morning noises met my ears. The sound of my aunt banging pans in the kitchen, the low hum of the Weather Channel's background music, the whine of a neighbor's lawn mower, the toilet lid slamming shut, and the whoosh of a flush. An ordinary day in a house with two kids and one adult who had witnessed a fierce dragon duel in a dank landfill filled with rats, cockroaches, maggots, dwarfs, dragons, and humans called cosantóirs. Normal, typical American stuff.

"I don't get it, Sissy. Like, why aren't Zach or Aunt Neece in here asking a million and one questions about last night? Am I the only one who remembers all of that?"

Sissy trilled and butted my hand for an ear scratch.

"You're no help." I gave Sissy another gentle pat. When I checked Grandmother Ivey's watch, the second hand still moved and the time was correct. But it had stopped last night. I saw it!

"It *did* happen. I *know* it did!" I went ahead and wound it a little anyway.

I flipped back the covers and padded down the hall with Sissy trailing behind. In the living room, the Weather Channel reported clear skies across the Deep South, with 60% humidity and a current temperature of 75°. The rainy spell had broken the spine of summer, and the forecasters boasted about the highs expected for the upcoming week, the low 90s or even, gasp, the upper 80s! Everyone would be in a better state of mind. But my mood felt sour, like the taste in the back of my mouth. Was J okay or were his injuries as horrible as I recalled? The thought he might not survive made me want to crawl back into bed and bury myself beneath layers of covers forever.

I waited in the hallway until Zach emerged from the bathroom. "Um, you okay?" I grasped his shoulders and stared into his eyes.

"Huh? What's your problem? Move already." He shoved off my hands and pushed past.

"Whatever." I took my turn in the bathroom. I brushed my teeth twice to rid my mouth of a stale taste that wouldn't seem to go away—dragon ale, had to be it.

A few minutes later, I slogged down the stairs and stood at the threshold of the sunroom. My shoulders sagged. The Rainy Day Box didn't wait on its usual perch atop the cedar chest.

"Where's the—?"

"—I stored it." Aunt Neece watched me from her position in front of the stove, a spatula in one hand.

The kitchen filled with the scent of turkey bacon, coffee, and pancakes. Zach moved browned cakes from Aunt Neece's growing stack to four plates already laden with bacon strips and nectarine sections. Drat. I was supposed to be Aunt Neece's chef-in-training. Wait, *four* plates? The doorbell rang before I could fire off questions.

"Please get that, Aidan," my great aunt said without looking up.

Miz Bridie stepped inside when I opened the front door. Her layered rainbow of skirts whirled around her. "Heard you were having some of those colorful pancakes your aunt is famous for." She ambled past, her cane tapping a rhythm. I tagged behind her to the kitchen. "I was in the neighborhood, and thought I'd drop by." She laughed hard. Like I'd really believe she'd just "happened" to pop in. Maybe that was it—Aunt Neece was waiting on Miz Bridie so we could talk about last night.

Zach dug into his pancakes as soon as we said *Amen*.

"Sure will miss these, Aunt Neece," he said. "Wish Mama could make 'em like this." A glob of pancake mush fell from his mouth and landed on his plate. Cane syrup shot onto the placemat.

I braced for a teachable moment about not talking with a mouth full of food, but Aunt Neece stared out the window and sipped her coffee. She hadn't touched her pancakes. And still nobody had said a word about the dragon fight.

Miz Bridie carried the conversation, flicking her gaze toward Aunt Neece from time to time. Her silver and gold wrist bangles clanged like wind chimes. She asked Zach about baseball and me about cheerleading and my writing.

She talked about when she was a little girl and what school subjects she had enjoyed. I ate in silence, other than when I answered one of her questions with as few words as possible.

Breakfast took twice as long this morning. We had nowhere to go but home. The things I really wanted to discuss, no one brought up. Like none of it had ever happened. Adults do that. The world can fall to a gazillion pieces and you can win the lottery or smash the car into a jagged hunk of metal, and they'll talk about the weather or what dress to wear or made-up people on some television show.

Aunt Neece glanced at the wall clock and motioned toward my brother. "Zach, let's do one final check of your duffle bag, then get you cleaned up and ready to go." She walked behind him with one push-hand midway of his back.

Good. Maybe now I could get some answers. Miz Bridie and I stacked the dishes and carried them to the sink.

It took a few minutes for the two of us to load the dishwasher, wipe the table, and scour the griddle. Still, she rambled on and on about useless stuff until I thought my head would explode. How could I get her to talk about *it*?

I opened the treat canister and doled out tuna bits for Mr. Pig and Sissy—the last they'd get from me 'til our next visit. They each ate four, then Mr. Pig trilled his thank-you and Sissy kissed my hand. I decided to love cats, and I knew what I wanted for my birthday. We had two slobbery black labs that mostly stayed in the fenced-in yard. I loved Toby and Butch, but a cat could sit on my bed while I wrote in my journal or beg for treats from a jar I'd keep in my room. And it would be all mine—although a cat is not as good as a dragon.

Too bad I couldn't have J. Other than needing an after-school job as a movie star to afford sushi, taking care of J would be a breeze. No litter box.

The silence unnerved me. So many questions needed answers, but I didn't know if I should ask. Better to start with something bland. "You have a strange name, Miz Bridie."

She chuckled. "Suppose I do. Doesn't sound odd to me, since I've lived with it for many lifetimes. It's an old Celtic name, passed down in my family for several generations. Bridie means *exalted one*."

Other people might see a slightly-bent woman who walked with a cane, but the way she had handled that mahogany dragon and saved the day, or night, "exalted one" worked for me.

Miz Bridie heated a cup of water in the microwave and brought it and a teabag to the table. That's when I noticed: the note I'd left last night for my aunt beneath the Mickey Mouse magnet was gone. I looked down and spotted Miz Bridie's red lace-up shoes, the same ones she'd worn to the dragon fight. It hadn't all been some crazy nightmare!

She didn't miss a thing. "You must feel fairly confused about last night, Aidan."

Finally, an adult ready to talk! I was all over it, but where to start? "Wackadoo is probably a better way to put it."

"Wackadoo? That's a new one for me." She gave a gentle laugh. "It will get easier to understand."

"Yeah, well, please explain it to me." I plopped down hard on a chair, rested my elbows on the table, and cupped my chin in my hands. "About that box and the landfill and that wild party last night." I took a breath and launched. "And why Aunt Neece went all blank and why she told us the wrong thing about lightning and thunder."

"Lightning and thunder?" Miz Bridie's auburn brows drew together.

"Aunt Neece knows about a lot of stuff and she's always doing these 'teachable moment' things when we're here. She told us thunder came first, then the lightning, but that's wrong. It's lightning first, then thunder because light travels faster than sound." I took a huge gulp of apple juice and almost choked. When I could continue, I said, "Why would she do that? Is she losing it?"

Miz Bridie looked at me, her eyebrows doing the question mark dance again. "And this bothers you more than all of the other things?"

I stared at her without blinking. So much of this bothered me. I hooked my ankles around the chair legs. "Seems like a good place to start."

"Your aunt isn't 'losing it,' not exactly." She sunk her teabag into the cup. "When you spend too much time in the Otherworld, life becomes—" Miz Bridie groped for a word "—tangled. The rules of nature, of everything, are at best confusing and often completely reversed. At one time, your Aunt Neece had difficulty separating the two realities." She placed her palms on the table. "It's a problem common to cosantóirs."

"And what about J? Is he okay? Aunt Neece hid the box and I can't even find out!"

She put a plump hand on top of mine. "J is fine, dear. Dragons possess an unsurpassed ability to heal themselves, as long as the injuries aren't overly severe."

I shifted my hand and held it up. "Wait."

I moved from the kitchen and peered down the hallway to make sure my brother and aunt weren't anywhere near, before I returned and sat down. "Aunt Neece hasn't said one word about anything since we got back," I said in a low voice. "And when she went all still and weird in the Great Hall—what was up with that?"

"My friend Denise passed through a dark time when she was just a few years older than you are now, sixteen or seventeen as I recall."

I leaned across the table and whispered, "What happened?"

"Not my tale, Aidan. She will share when she feels the time is right." Miz Bridie held up one finger. "A person's deepest pain belongs to that person." She tapped her chin with the finger. "I can tell you this. She had an association with the ebony dragon for a while. Shaking one's demon is a triumph. Facing that same demon later is another." She paused, then added, "Sometimes, the adults in your life can't help you, Aidan. Even the ones who love you from here to the ends of the Otherworld."

I got up and poured myself a cup of coffee. In two months, I would be thirteen. High time to drink the adult beverage preferred by my mother and aunt. Maybe it would make me feel less like a zombie. Help me understand all this heavy stuff.

I took one sip, winced. Awful, worse than that swampy dragon ale! I poured out some, added milk and two teaspoons of sugar, and stirred. The second sip wasn't *as* bad. Coffee would take some getting used to. Maybe that's why Malcolm and Miz Bridie preferred tea.

"What is this business about dragon guardians?" I asked. "I don't get that either."

She dunked her teabag up and down a few more times, then squished the bag against the spoon, squeezing out the last bit. "When you're thirteen—"

"What is the big hairy deal about turning thirteen? Thirteen is so... nothing!" Frustration boiled up in me, like I might spew all over the kitchen, doing worse damage than J's sneeze-uls had done to the sunroom walls. I stared into the cup in my hand. Did coffee do that to a person—make them all rude and messed up? I bet with some of that cassina black drink the Apalachee natives made, I could stomp thirty dragons into the landfill mud.

"Thirteen?" Miz Bridie measured a teaspoon of Tupelo honey into her teacup, stirred, and tasted before answering. "Thirteen is everything, Aidan. Thirteen is the age when a young cosantóir receives her first, and hopefully only, dragon."

"Are you saying I'll get a dragon for my birthday?" Miles better than a cat! Not that I wouldn't mind having both.

But Miz Bridie held a finger to her lips. Aunt Neece and Zach were coming down the hall.

CHAPTER FIFTEEN

Aunt Neece concentrated on her driving while I played an annoying word game with Zach. The leftover relief at seeing him appear last night in the Great Hall and getting all mushy about being his big sister had worn thin, big-time. One good thing about going home: he could go to his room with his computer and tech junk and I could escape to mine, to rest my ears and think. I had a door and I would use it. No mouthy little brother allowed.

"I'm in Delaware with Donna eating doughnuts," Zach said. "Your turn, Aunt Neece."

"Guess I can play and avoid semis at the same time," she said. "What do I have to do again?"

"Say a place, then a person's name, then what they're eating," I answered. "Next letter in line. You're *E*."

"That's a hard one. Hmm... I'm in England with Elvis eating éclairs."

"Good one, Aunt Neece. I'm in France with Francine eating French fries." I flipped around to jab a finger at my brother in the back seat. "Go, G!"

"I'm in Georgia with Gina eating..." Zach kicked the back of Aunt Neece's seat while he thought. She shot him the calm-down eye in the rearview mirror. He stopped. "Eating... grapes!"

Aunt Neece caught on fast. “I’m in Helsinki with Harold eating horseradish.” She exited from the Interstate and hit the connector road to take us to Highway 27 south. I liked this road much better than the crowded Interstate. At least there were houses and cows to see along the way.

As we continued the word game, I noticed several large black birds soaring in wide circles high above the treetops: buzzards looking for a fresh roadkill lunch. I’d never seen them up close, only clustered around some mound of yuck, picking off chunks. Like maggots, a necessary, disgusting part of the life and death cycle.

“Go, Aidan!” Zach called out.

“Inside voice, sir. We’re in the front seat, not in Australia,” Aunt Neece said.

“What letter?” I asked.

“You’re *I*! Pay attention.” Zach pulled a frown.

I stuck out my tongue. “I’m in... Indonesia with Ida eating... eating...” My overtaxed brain blanked out. Probably the lack of sleep. Normally, I excelled with words.

“Hah! You’re out, out, out.” Zach celebrated. I wanted to thump him on the head.

I shrugged and stared from the window at the scenery—nothing now but miles and miles of oak and pine trees lining a grassy state highway. Until I spotted more buzzards.

Seven, I counted, with others joining the looping aerial circus. Must’ve been something huge to draw such a flock, maybe a deer unlucky enough to have tangled with a speeding car. One bird broke free from the queue and flew in our direction, dipping lower and lower until it was less than two car lengths in front of us. I gasped. It ascended and lowered its feet, more like a hawk on the hunt than a scavenger. Seconds before it reached the windshield, it retracted its talons and jerked up, barely missing the hood.

"Yowza!" I jerked around and craned my head to follow its receding path. "Did you see that?"

Aunt Neece looked over. "See what?"

"It's not your turn, Aidan," Zach said, Mr. Don't Mess Up My Fun. "You lost. Now it's between me and Aunt Neece."

I ignored him. "That buzzard. It nearly hit us!"

Aunt Neece glanced from the road, to me, back to the road. I searched the sky. No birds. None!

"I must've missed it," she said.

The game continued, now between Zach and my aunt. She named exotic places, made up silly names and food I had never heard of, but he hung in there. A few minutes passed. The trees lining the highway yielded to cleared pastureland spotted with a few cows, goats, and the occasional horse. I kept an eye out for buzzards, but for a while there were none.

I was beginning to think me seeing those birds must've been like when a thirsty man thinks he spots an oasis in a desert—I didn't get a whole lot of sleep, maybe my brain was fried—when a sharp movement to my right caught my attention. I jerked my head in time to see a buzzard heading toward my side, in line with the passenger-side window. Before I could speak, five more appeared, in a tight V-formation like the Blue Angel fighter jets. Buzzards didn't do that, did they? They rode the thermals, exerting as little energy as possible. We had covered that factoid at Camp Neece one year.

My vision blurred and the car around me faded. I could still hear the dim murmur of voices. Zach saying, "Quincy with Que-Que eating Quinces," and Aunt Neece laughing.

The buzzards flew at my window. Their jagged wings beat against the glass. Impossible, we were going too fast for that!

Their knobby red beaks jabbed the window. I saw flashes of mean eyes and waxy black feathers. One claw extended forward, then passed unharmed through the pane, aiming for my face. I threw up my hands.

"Aidan?" Aunt Neece said.

I blinked. No buzzards. The sky remained clear of clouds, the light blue of late summer. "Wha..."

"It's your turn," Zach said. "I won, Aunt Neece missed. New game. You have A, for Aidan."

When Aunt Neece pulled her car into the parking lot for Sullivan's Kitchen, a country restaurant near the midpoint between Lake City and Tallahassee, I spotted our white behemoth SUV. Daddy and Mama! It had only been four days since I had seen them, but it seemed like decades. So much had happened. Zach bounded from the back seat, almost before the car came to a halt.

Good thing they had driven *the beast*. Mama's car, an old Honda famous for its gas mileage but little else, barely had room for all of our luggage and us. Zach never kept his feet on his side, and he would've tormented me all the way to Lake City.

Zach ran up to the SUV's driver's side window, jumping and jiving like he didn't have good sense. Daddy got out, then Mama. They formed a hug triangle. Hey, what about me?

I jabbed at my seat belt release and it wouldn't let me go. Zach walked between our parents, his head pivoting to one then the other, talking and talking and talking. Mama glanced back once, gave a small wave, and they disappeared into the little eatery. They didn't love me anymore. What had I done? Then it ding-a-donged. This was a set-up: one of those adult maneuvers so Aunt Neece and I would have a few moments alone. Did Aunt Neece have some superpower to freeze my seatbelt?

I swiveled to look at her, eyebrows lifted. She smiled. "Nothing gets past you, does it?" She pushed the release on her belt. It popped open. Then mine did. Just like that.

"A lot gets past me," I said. Like Charity and her poor little bad girl act. To think I had given her my only San Luis Mission shirt.

Aunt Neece stared out the window for a moment, twirling her silver ring. Though I'd seen it many times, I finally understood the strange green stone. "Is that—?"

She nodded. "It's one of J's scale tips. I had it fashioned into a ring so I could keep it near." The car idled. The vents pushed chilled air onto my flushed face. "I'm sure J gave you one, too. Dragons like to do that. I feel better, keeping mine close. I know a talented jewelry artist, in case you ever want one made, or maybe a pendant. I could have your shard mounted for your thirteenth birthday."

I didn't reply, but I felt the reassuring shape of the dragon shard in my cargo pocket. A necklace would work, one with a long chain so I could wear it under my shirt, close to my heart. Wouldn't have to take it off for cheerleading.

She sighed. "There's so much to tell you, Aidan. I don't know where to start."

"Just dig in, Aunt Neece. That's what Mama tells me to do."

When she laughed, the tiny worry lines around her mouth turned into dimples. She threaded her fingers through her red hair and it stuck up on top like a Mohawk. "In two months, I'll turn J's box and the dragon cosantóir job over to you."

"Why me?"

A hawk landed on a dead limb, high in a tree. It stared down at our car. Glad it wasn't a buzzard. Dragonflies flitted through the tall grass, dragons hiding in plain sight.

"You are from a long line of cosantóirs, women who are entrusted with guarding the dragons that remain. Dragon Rules dictate that these guardians are always female, and from every other generation. In rare situations, a male or someone from outside of the chosen bloodline might become a cosantóir by default, but not often. Takes the full consent of the High Council of Masters for that."

High Council of Masters? Dragon Rules? This was way more involved than anything I could imagine. My brain hurt.

"Men and boys traditionally play roles as protectors because of their natural strength, their bravado." She tapped her temple then pointed to me. "But females are selected for the honor of becoming cosantóirs for their wily ways, their intuition."

"A little sexist, Aunt Neece." Mama used those same words, "a little sexist," whenever someone declared she *had* to do a thing, or *not* do a thing, just because she was a woman.

Aunt Neece chuckled. "Suppose it is. Women have come a long way, especially in this part of the world." She sighed. "In others, not so much. Dragon Rules make sense, in part, because of the innate abilities of females and males. Sure, you may train and become as strong as your frame will allow. Still, given a few years and a good dose of male hormones, Zach will outreach you in some capacities. No denying nature. One day, Zach will help you in ways you can't imagine now."

Right-O, Aunt Neece. I couldn't fathom it. Zach stronger than me? Hah! I could flatten him if I needed to. I snapped the seat belt aside, but now I didn't want to get out.

"Our cosantóir lineage comes from your great-great grandmother's side of the family, passed down through the Ivey clan females," she continued. "We can trace it back many generations, through war, peace, famine, and wealth. Then further, to a time before written records." She took a sip from her bottled water. "A lot of the history is murky, the stuff of oral legends, and we have no way to pinpoint exactly when the box and J's morph came into our possession."

"Why not let the world know? I mean, we could have J and the others declared endangered or something."

"Wouldn't work. The dragons that have chosen not to shift permanently to dainties possess far too much power, too much knowledge. Terrible, bloody wars have been fought for less. Humans have always feared what they don't understand." She took a deep breath, blew it out. "I need, and want, to apologize to you, Aidan."

"For what?"

"I never intended for you or Zach to become..." She paused. Tears formed in her eyes. One slid down her cheek and she brushed it away.

The only times I'd ever seen her cry was over chopped onions and when that lady died in the car crash on Her Show.

Aunt Neece sat. I waited.

"I should've just taken you to a safe spot over there, let you meet J," she continued. "Should've never allowed you to touch that box by yourself before you came into your cosantóir position." She reached over and gave my hand an affectionate pat. "I thought you might benefit from meeting J ahead of time on neutral ground—a little get-acquainted visit in the safety of *my* house—before it all got dumped in your lap." She paused to flick her eyes up and grin. "Even if it meant I had to repaint my sunroom." My great aunt grew solemn again. "I never, not in a million years, thought you'd end up in the dark dragon's lair. Tell me everything that happened, Aidan. It's important."

I gave her the flash-quick version, from J's first appearance, to the smoky mirror in the Capitol, the grocery store incident, to Charity, the dragon in the Mission church, to the landfill and Malcolm. The black van, the buzzard attack, the snakes: All of it came tumbling out.

I felt tons lighter, but it seemed as if the weight was on her now. Her face clouded for a moment. She slumped over the wheel before she took a deep breath and said, "Charity is what we cosantóirs refer to as a *disruptive*. She draws others into her shadowy, troubled world. Always a cart in the ditch, a loved one in immediate, grave danger." Aunt Neece's features grew stern. "A person can get caught up in the drama, the moods, the needs. There are disruptives in this life, and in the Otherworld. Disruptive entities distract you from your true purpose, your true path, by sucking all of your energy to use as their own."

I stared down at my tanned knees. She'd sure summed up Charity. Was the blonde fairy really her sister, or had that whole thing been a clever act? Two-faced, that's what we called that kind of girl at school. And I didn't get to meet their other bizarre sister Hope.

"But I don't get it, Aunt Neece. Why did Charity treat me like that? Besides, aren't Faith, Hope, and Charity the names of the three virtues, as in *good* ways to act?"

"Yes, those are virtues all humans need to hold dear. But names are names, and those three had theirs long before they became what they now are." She sighed. "I have always sought to have the answers for you and your brother."

"Teachable moments. Just not ones about dragons and fairies." I cocked my head to one side and raised my eyebrows.

Aunt Neece offered a slight smile and nod before her face went all serious again. "When it comes to the Otherworld, I have few answers to give you, the basics really. Maybe someday, Charity's motives will become clear. For now, I'd stay as far away from her as possible. Disruptives can ruin your life." Her fingers fiddled with the ring again. "I had my own disruptive. His name was Jermaine."

"What happened?"

"Maybe when you're older. Not now." When Aunt Neece noticed my disgusted look, she gave another little smile. "I fell into the trap of living too much over there—," she made a broad sweeping motion with her hands then patted the seat, "—and not enough here, and it almost destroyed me. I still don't sleep much, even after all the time that has passed." She shimmed her shoulders as if she shook off sadness. "I've learned to nap. Suppose you noticed that."

People always told me how I'm old for my age, or as Mama put it, *Aidan, you were born thirty.* Because I entertained deep thoughts? Because my vocabulary outshone most of my friends'? I'd rather learn an interesting new word a day than eat a bowl of chocolate ice cream. Well, almost.

Right now, this dragon guardian stuff felt like a boulder the size of a dragon, squashing me down. And I wished maybe I wasn't so deep.

"I know you'll have more questions, Aidan. We can talk again, soon."

I held up a stop-finger. "Please, just a couple more." I pulled aside my hair to reveal my birthmark. "What's up with this? You have one too."

"It's the brand mark of our dragon. Everyone in a bloodline has one, even the ones who will never become cosantóirs. Buys all of us a small amount of protection, especially those who enter the Otherworld."

I'd have to check Mama, Zach, Aunt Sarah, and my little cousin. "And why did you say *serpent energy* when I told you about that snake at Wakulla Springs?"

"Didn't realize you heard that." Her red eyebrows did their jiggle dance. "Cosantóirs possess an odd kind of glamour, a sparkle that reptiles can sense—snakes, lizards, alligators—even an occasional non-reptile, like a frog, worm, or caterpillar, and of course, all the dragons in disguise. You'll have more encounters like that one." She considered. "Not a bad thing, really. They will sense you as a friend, as long as you don't challenge or threaten them." She paused. "Actually, you must have a double dose. Most dragon guardians don't shimmer until after they officially inherit the role."

So... that explained the reptile audience at the Mission council house. I scribbled another reminder in my to-do list: review snake markings, especially the venomous varieties. Boy was my mental notepad filling up.

"It's not *really* a Rainy Day Box, is it?" I asked.

"No. I made that up. As I said earlier, a mistake on my part. What I believed to be a clever way to allow you to meet your dragon."

"But the landfill fight stopped when the rain did."

"Difficult to explain that. Probably your intent working. You *thought* our side of reality controlled the Otherworld. No rain meant no dragons, no landfill. Intent means a lot in the

Otherworld, but not always. The rules, and *time* as we know it, are slippery over there. You'll understand more... later."

Aunt Neece switched off the air conditioner and hit the toggles to lower the windows. Outside air filtered in, drier, with a hint of change. The weather was deceitful, like Charity, teasing of chilly evenings and color-dappled leaves and football games. More heat would come. It always did, until autumn finally shoved it aside and took charge.

Weariness squeezed my foggy brain. I didn't want to think about evil dragons or vile landfills or dragon guardians or intentions. Why couldn't cheerleading and writing and clothes be enough? I was still a kid, at least for two more months.

I felt my pocket for J's scale. Still there. "Aunt Neece, I kind of lied to you a couple of days ago." So much for cleaning toilets and self-imposed penance.

"I know."

I stared at her. "Really?"

"To protect J. Yes, I know you did it for that reason alone." She fixed me with an intense stare. "You know how I feel about lying, but I understand. If you decide to accept the mantle of cosantóir—and you *do* have the right to refuse—there will be times when you have to hide, to tell half-truths, sometimes complete lies."

Sure I could fudge a bit, here and there. But keep a dragon? Could I do that?

Aunt Neece's face looked even more tired, as if she'd traveled for miles and miles without a break, but then she lifted her chin. "Confidence... that's all it takes."

Confidence in my art. Confidence in my writing and cheerleading. Piece of pie with whipped cream and a cherry on top. But this? I slipped my hand into my pocket to touch

J's scale tip. It felt warm against my fingers. "I *can* handle it, Aunt Neece."

"I do believe you can." She looked at me, all serious-faced. "You must promise me this, Aidan. When it comes to the guardian box and J, I am the one person you must always trust, must come to if you have a problem. Don't try to tackle everything alone." She paused, took a deep breath, and let it out. "I know I didn't exactly live up to my guardian role recently, but I have finally moved past meeting the dark dragon again face to face, and I feel as if I can go back to the Otherworld, when, and if, you need me. As soon as it's official, there will be other people—"

"Like Miz Bridie?"

"Yes. Bridie and her dragon K, among many others. Miz Bridie is more, much more. She's what they call a Master Cosantóir. A *very* old and wise person." She chuckled. "Bridie is, as you like to say, about a *gazillion* times more powerful than I could ever be. But you'll learn much more about her when you turn thirteen." She clasped her hands. "It will be the most amazing adventure." For a moment, her eyes lost their weariness and sparkled. "Secret meetings, coded words, sacred spots in this world and the Otherworld where only cosantóirs and their dragons can go." She paused. "Plus a handful of other mystical creatures you can't even imagine."

"I can write about it in my journal. This will be *so* awesome."

"I don't think that would be wise, Aidan."

"Hiding in plain sight, Aunt Neece. Don't you get it? If I write it like it's a fantasy, no one will believe it's really true."

"Still, not wise." She wagged a finger at me. "And no more drawings of things you see over there either."

"So *you* took them. Not cool!"

Aunt Neece nodded. "I'm sorry. I had to." She rippled one hand through her hair. The birthmark flashed for a moment, before the hair fell back over it. "Be careful, Aidan. I worry. The dark omens—that van, the shadows, the buzzards—could mean that you're on the ebony dragon's radar. For some reason, probably connected somehow to Charity, he has taken keen notice of you, and that's not good. I had one visit from an annoying crow before I became a cosantóir, but he only cawed a few times and flapped around."

My aunt studied me for a long pause, her eyes watering again. "You've always been special to me, Aidan, since the first time I held you at the hospital right after you were born. You with that thatch of bright red fuzz so like mine." She reached over and touched my hair. "And the tiny cosantóir mark on your little neck, so precious. I've tried not to play favorites with you, my redheaded dragon-guardian niece, but I couldn't help it. I see so much of me in you." She took a shaky breath. "J will be in good hands. I know you'll navigate this with much more care than I managed."

"So J was your dragon?"

"For a time, yes. But I was never the cosantóir I know you have the potential to be, should you choose." She turned to stare from the front window, a faraway look in her eyes. "There's so much you don't yet know, *can't* know, until you are a proper guardian." She swiveled toward me. "It is a wonderous life, sometimes frightening, but the most rewarding duty a human could ever hope for. It is more than a family legacy. It is the one true thing you have dreamed of since you were born. Am I correct?"

I nodded. My first memory was of looking out through white-painted slats at the shimmery outline of a tiny green dragon. Years later, when I shared this with my mom, she had given a small laugh and assured me, "An infant doesn't possess the developmental capacity for such detailed recall." My mom and her Nurse Language.

But the drawings, seeing dragons at every turn, both awake and in my dreams? It *had* all meant something!

Aunt Neece nodded toward the restaurant. "We should go in. Your brother is probably on his second order of fries by now."

"Do Mama and Daddy know about this whole dragon thing?"

"Your daddy knows we have a family secret. Your mother knows, of course. I took her into the Otherworld when she was younger, to a meadow I like to visit. One of the few truly safe places for a non-cosantóir." Aunt Neece turned the key and pocketed it. "Your Aunt Sarah never showed an interest so she's never crossed over with me. Still, it's not a topic we openly discuss." She fixed me with a stern look. "And we *never, ever* disclose anything to outsiders."

Aunt Neece slid from the driver's side and got out. I watched her walk away. On my wrist, Grandmother Ivey's battered old watch marked off time with a tick, tick, tick. The tiny green shards beside the dial caught the light and glittered. Now I knew what they were, too. At least a few things made sense. I wasn't a lunatic for seeing dragons at every turn.

I pictured myself seated on a floating log, rolling down some zigzagging river, pushed along by forces below and above.

But for now, I'd be starting eighth grade.

How about you, Aidan? I imagined Olivia the Perfect drilling me about my time away from the cheerleading squad. *What did you do on your summer vacay?*

I ate sushi with a green dragon, befriended a homeless, two-faced, dark fair-a-tude, sipped lemongrass tea with a dwarf in a landfill, and managed a prime spot on the stalker list of an ebony dragon. Nothing special.

Like either Zach or I could confess the truth, even if he could remember any of it. I opened my door and followed my great aunt into Sullivan's, anticipating a huge crock of their creamy mac and cheese. Maybe I'd order more than one.

I could ace any class, even the ones I didn't particularly like. I could cook better than people way older than me. I taught myself how to draw and paint before I could write. If I could keep Zach out of trouble, I could do anything.

Even watch over a dragon.

How hard could it be?

I had two whole months to decide whether to accept the guardian role, or not.

And a whole new set of regulations:

The Dragon Rules.

DRAGON CUISINE

Aidan's Wacko Nachos

Human version:

1 jar salsa (any kind, mild or hot)

Greek yogurt, plain, non–fat

Shredded sharp cheddar cheese

Tortilla chips

On a microwave-safe plate, spread out tortilla chips. Top each chip with a dollop of Greek yogurt, a little salsa, and a pinch or two of shredded cheddar cheese. Heat in microwave for 20-30 seconds until cheese melts.

Yummo!

Dragon version:

Prepare as above, except...for a sushi-loving dragon, you can use a little tuna on top before you finish off with the cheese.

Aunt Neece's Confetti Pancakes

Ingredients

1 ½ cups all-purpose flour

3 ½ teaspoons baking powder

1 teaspoon salt

1 Tablespoon white sugar

3 Tablespoons butter, melted

1 egg

1 ¼ cups milk (I use 2%)

1 Tablespoon confetti candy sprinkles (more or less to taste)

Cooking spray

Directions

Sift together flour, baking powder, salt and sugar in a large bowl.

Whisk in melted butter, egg, and milk until combined. Let the batter rest for 5 minutes.

Add the candy sprinkles and mix in.

Preheat a large skillet or flat griddle over medium-high heat. Spray with cooking spray. Ladle batter onto the skillet. An ice cream scoop for each pancake makes the perfect size. Cook for 2 to 3 minutes until you see little bubbles appearing on the sides and center of each pancake. Flip and cook until golden brown, about 1 to 2 minutes.

Serve hot with butter and syrup (barely warm syrup in a small pitcher in microwave, about 15 seconds).

Fast Method

If you don't have time to make the batter from scratch, you can make the batter using:

2 cups pancake mix

1 cup milk

2 eggs

1 Tablespoon of confetti candy sprinkles

Mix together, then cook as above.

THANK YOU FOR READING
THE DRAGON BOX!

Please take a short moment to leave an online review or star rating. Reviews are invaluable to indie authors, and each one is greatly appreciated!

ABOUT THE AUTHOR

Rhett DeVane is the author of several middle grade chapter books, as well as eight mainstream fiction novels, two coauthored novels, short stories, flash fiction, and poetry.

Rhett's stories have won numerous awards from the Tallahassee Writers Association, the Florida Writers Association, and the Florida Authors and Publishers Association.

For the past forty-plus years, Rhett has made her home in Tallahassee, located in Florida's Big Bend area, where she splits her time between writing and thinking about writing. She is currently working on multiple middle grade and young adult stories, because her muses refuse to contain her in a single box.

Learn more at **www.rhettdevane.com**

Author photo © Lance Oliver, Lance Oliver Photography. Used by permission.

Coming Soon
From Author Rhett DeVane:

DRAGON RULES

—Book Two of the Dragon Guardians Series!

The day Aidan McAllister turned thirteen, she became a dragon guardian, a cosantóir, for J, a powerful and somewhat goofy green dragon. Being a cosantóir is not all fun and games. The rules of J's Otherworld shift on a whim, and danger lurks at every turn. When her little brother Zach takes off with J on an Otherworld misadventure, Aidan enlists the help of Paige Gauley to rescue Zach, bending important Dragon Rules. Aidan vows to do everything in her power to protect Zach, J, and Paige, a true friend she now thinks of as her cosantóir sister.

Look for *Dragon Rules* coming in 2026!

Visit **www.happycatpress.com** and sign up for our newsletter to get the latest Dragon news, download freebies, stay informed about release dates, and more!

Also From Happy Cat Press:

Want More Dragons?

You'll Love

Drakin the Dragon and the Quest for Strawberries

Written and Illustrated by **Cristen Elizabeth Rose**

Drakin just wants to make the perfect strawberry cake for his unicorn friend Spike's birthday, but gathering ingredients leads to a midnight misunderstanding at the royal palace. When a curious princess, a determined guard, and a one flustered dragon meet in the Blue Mist Mountains, suspicion turns into friendship, and a birthday surprise becomes pure magic.

A beautifully hand-illustrated tale of courage, kindness, and unexpected friendship. Perfect for ages 6–10.

Visit **www.happycatpress.com** to learn more.

About the Publisher

At Happy Cat Press, we are conjurers of the curious and creators of wonder. We craft books and artful oddities for those who still believe in secret doors and half-forgotten names. We dream in ink and delight in the rustle of a page turned by candlelight.

Don't miss a single whisker-twitching tale or curious delight. Sign up for the Happy Cat Press Gazette! Straight from the inkwell of Sir T. Critterby, you'll receive periodic dispatches brimming with bookish secrets, printable oddities, and enchanting news from the Parlor. Adventure awaits—come along for the wonder!

Sign up and get free stuff! ☞
www.happycatpress.com

www.ingramcontent.com/pod-product-compliance
Lightning Source LLC
LaVergne TN
LVHW010913110826
845149LV00013B/2346

* 9 7 9 8 9 8 8 5 1 5 9 3 7 *